Susanna & Sue

Kate Douglas Smith Wiggin

Copyright © 2023 Culturea Editions
Text and cover : © public domain
Edition : Culturea (Hérault, 34)
Contact : infos@culturea.fr
Print in Germany by Books on Demand
Design and layout : Derek Murphy
Layout : Reedsy (https://reedsy.com/)
ISBN : 9791041826902
Légal deposit : July 2023
All rights reserved

Susanna and Sue

I

IT was the end of May, when "spring goeth all in white." The apple trees were scattering their delicate petals on the ground, dropping them over the stone walls to the roadsides, where in the moist places of the shadows they fell on beds of snowy innocence. Here and there a single tree was tinged with pink, but so faintly, it was as if the white were blushing. Now and then a tiny white butterfly danced in the sun and pearly clouds strayed across the sky in fleecy flocks.

Everywhere the grass was of ethereal greenness, a greenness drenched with the pale yellow of spring sunshine. Looking from earth to sky and from blossom to blossom, the little world of the apple orchards, shedding its falling petals like fair-weather snow, seemed made of alabaster and porcelain, ivory and mother-of-pearl, all shimmering on a background of tender green.

After you pass Albion village, with its streets shaded by elms and maples and its outskirts embowered in blossoming orchards, you wind along a hilly country road that runs between grassy fields. Here the whiteweed is already budding, and there are pleasant pastures dotted with rocks and fringed with spruce and fir; stretches of woodland, too, where the road is lined with giant pines and you lift your face gratefully to catch the cool balsam breath of the forest. Coming from out this splendid shade, this silence too deep to be disturbed by light breezes or vagrant winds, you find yourself on the brow of a descending hill. The first thing that strikes the eye is a lake that might be a great blue sapphire dropped into the verdant hollow where it lies. When the eye reluctantly leaves the lake on the left, it turns to rest upon the little Shaker Settlement on the right—a dozen or so large comfortable white barns, sheds, and houses, standing in the wide orderly spaces of their own spreading acres of farm and timber land. There again the spring goeth all in white, for there is no spot to fleck the dazzling quality of Shaker paint, and their apple, plum, and pear trees are so well cared for that the snowy blossoms are fairly hiding the branches.

The place is very still, although there are signs of labor in all directions. From a window of the girls' building a quaint little gray-clad figure is beating a braided rug; a boy in homespun, with his hair slightly long in the back and cut in a straight line across the forehead, is carrying milk-cans from the dairy to one of the Sisters' Houses. Men in broad-brimmed hats, with clean-shaven, ascetic faces, are ploughing or harrowing here and there in thefields, while a group of Sisters is busy setting out plants and vines in some beds near a cluster of noble trees. That cluster of trees, did the eye of the stranger realize it, was the very starting-point of this Shaker Community, for in the year , the valiant Father James Whittaker, one of Mother Ann Lee's earliest English converts, stopped near the village of Albion on his first visit to Maine. As he and his Elders alighted from their horses, they stuck into the ground the willow withes they had used as whips, and now, a hundred years later, the trees that had grown from these slender branches were nearly three feet in diameter.

From whatever angle you look upon the Settlement, the first and strongest impression is of quiet order, harmony, and a kind of austere plenty. Nowhere is the purity of the spring so apparent. Nothing is out of place; nowhere is any confusion, or appearance of loose ends, or neglected tasks. As you come nearer, you feel the more surely that here there has never been undue haste nor waste; no shirking, no putting off till the morrow what should have been done to-day. Whenever a shingle or a clapboard was needed it was put on, where paint was required it was used,—that is evident; and a look at the great barns stored with hay shows how the fields have been conscientiously educated into giving a full crop.

To such a spot as this might any tired or sinful heart come for rest; hoping somehow, in the midst of such frugality and thrift, such self-denying labor, such temperate use of God's good gifts, such shining cleanliness of outward things, to regain and wear "the white flower of a blameless life." The very air of the place breathed peace, so thought Susanna Hathaway; and little Sue, who skipped by her side, thought nothing at all save that she was with mother in the country; that it had been rather a sad journey, with mother so quiet and pale, and that she would be very glad to see supper,should it rise like a fairy banquet in the midst of these strange surroundings.

It was only a mile and a half from the railway station to the Shaker Settlement, and Susanna knew the road well, for she had driven over it more than once as child and girl. A boy would bring the little trunk that contained their simple necessities later on in the evening, so she and Sue would knock at the door of the house where visitors were admitted, and be undisturbed by any gossiping company while they were pleading their case.

"Are we most there, Mardie?" asked Sue for the twentieth time. "Look at me! I'm being a butterfly, or perhaps a white pigeon. No, I'd rather be a butterfly, and then I can skim along faster and move my wings!"

The airy little figure, all lightness and brightness, danced along the road, the white cotton dress rising and falling, the white-stockinged legs much in evidence, the arms outstretched as if in flight, straw hat falling off yellow hair, and a little wisp of swansdown scarf floating out behind like the drapery of a baby Mercury.

"We are almost there," her mother answered. "You can see the buildings now, if you will stop being a butterfly. Don't you like them?"

"Yes, I 'specially like them all so white. Is it a town, Mardie?"

"It is a village, but not quite like other villages. I have told you often about the Shaker Settlement, where your grandmother brought me once when I was just your age. There was a thunder-storm; they kept us all night, and were so kind that I never forgot them. Then your grandmother and I stopped off once when we were going to Boston. I was ten then, and I remember more about it. The same sweet Eldress was there both times."

"What is an El-der-ess, Mardie?"

"A kind of everybody's mother, she seemed to be," Susanna responded, with a catch in her breath.

"I'd 'specially like her; will she be there now, Mardie?"

"I'm hoping so, but it is eighteen years ago. I was ten and she was about forty, I should think."

"Then o' course she'll be dead," said Sue, cheerfully, "or either she'll have no teeth or hair."

"People don't always die before they are sixty, Sue."

"Do they die when they want to, or when they must?"

"Always when they must; never, never when they want to," answered Sue's mother.

"But o' course they wouldn't ever *want* to if they had any little girls to be togedder with, like you and me, Mardie?" And Sue looked up with eyes that were always like two interrogation points, eager by turns and by turns wistful, but never satisfied.

"No," Susanna replied brokenly, "of course they wouldn't, unless sometimes they were wicked for a minute or two and forgot."

"Do the Shakers shake all the time, Mardie, or just once in a while? And shall I see them do it?"

"Sue, dear, I can't explain everything in the world to you while you are so little; you really must wait until you're more grown up. The Shakers don't shake and the Quakers don't quake, and when you're older, I'll try to make you understand why they were called so and why they kept the name."

"Maybe the El-der-ess can make me understand right off now; I'd 'specially like it." And Sue ran breathlessly along to the gate where the North Family House stood in its stately, white-and-green austerity.

Susanna followed, and as she caught up with the impetuous Sue, the front door of the house opened and a figure appeared on the threshold. Mother and child quickened their pace and went up the steps, Susanna with a hopeless burden of fear and embarrassment clogging her tongue and dragging at her feet; Sue so expectant of new disclosures and fresh experiences that her face beamed like a full moon.

Eldress Abby (for it was Eldress Abby) had indeed survived the heavy weight of her fifty-five or sixty summers, and looked as if she might reach a yet greater age. She wore the simple Shaker afternoon dress of drab alpaca; an irreproachable muslin surplice encircled her straight, spare shoulders, while her hair was almost entirely concealed by the stiffly wired, transparent white-net cap that served as a frame to the tranquil face. The face itself was a network of delicate, fine wrinkles; but every wrinkle must have been as lovely in God's sight as it was in poor unhappy Susanna Hathaway's. Some of them were graven by self-denial and hard work; others perhaps meant the giving up of home, of parents and brothers or sisters; perhaps some worldly love, the love that Father Adam bequeathed to the human family, had been slain in Abby's youth, and the scars still remained to show the body's suffering and the spirit's triumph. At all events, whatever foes had menaced her purity or her tranquillity had been conquered, and she exhaled serenity as the rose sheds fragrance.

"Do you remember the little Nelson girl and her mother that stayed here all night, years ago?" asked Susanna, putting out her hand timidly.

"DO YOU REMEMBER THE LITTLE
NELSON GIRL AND HER MOTHER?"

"Why, seems to me I do," assented Eldress Abby, genially. "So many comes and goes it's hard to remember all. Didn't you come once in a thunder-storm?"

"Yes, one of your barns was struck by lightning and we sat up all night."

"Yee, yee. I remember well! Your mother was a beautiful spirit. I couldn't forget her."

"And we came once again, mother and I, and spent the afternoon with you, and went strawberrying in the pasture."

"Yee, yee, so we did; I hope your mother continues in health."

"She died the very next year," Susanna answered in a trembling voice, for the time of explanation was near at hand and her heart failed her.

"Won't you come into the sitting-room and rest awhile? You must be tired walking from the deepot."

"No, thank you, not just yet. I'll step into the front entry a minute.—Sue, run and sit in that rocking-chair on the porch and watch the cows going into the big barn.—Do you remember, Eldress Abby, the second time I came, how you sat me down in the kitchen with a bowl of wild strawberries to hull for supper? They were very small and ripe; I did my best, for I never meant to be careless, but the bowl slipped and fell,—my legs were too short to reach the floor, and I couldn't make a lap,—so in trying to pick up the berries I spilled juice on my dress, and on the white apron you hadtied on for me. Then my fingers were stained and wet and the hulls kept falling in with the soft berries, and when you came in and saw me you held up your hands and said, 'Dear, dear! you *have* made a mess of your work!' Oh, Eldress Abby, they've come back to me all day, those words. I've tried hard to be good, but somehow I've made just such a mess of my life as I made of hulling the berries. The bowl is broken, I haven't much fruit to show, and I am all stained and draggled. I shouldn't have come to Albion on the five-o'clock train—that was an accident; I meant to come at noon, when you could turn me away if you wanted to."

"Nay, that is not the Shaker habit," remonstrated Abby. "You and the child can sleep in one of the spare chambers at the Office Building and be welcome."

"But I want much more than that," said Susanna, tearfully. "I want to come and live here, where there is no marrying nor giving in marriage. I am so tired with my disappointments and discouragements and failures that it is no use to try any longer. I am Mrs. Hathaway, and Sue is my child, but I have left my husband for good and all, and I only want to spend the rest of my days here in peace and bring up Sue to a more tranquil life than I have ever had. I have a little money, so that I shall not be a burden to you, and I will work from morning to night at any task you set me."

"I will talk to the Family," said Eldress Abby, gravely; "but there are a good many things to settle before we can say yee to all you ask."

"Let me confess everything freely and fully," pleaded Susanna, "and if you think I'm to blame, I will go away at once."

"Nay, this is no time for that. It is our duty to receive all and try all; then if you should be gathered in, you would unburden your heart to God through the Sister appointed to receive your confession."

"Will Sue have to sleep in the children's building away from me?"

"Nay, not now; you are company, not a Shaker, and anyway you could keep the child with you till she is a little older; that's not forbidden at first, though there comes a time when the ties of the flesh must be broken! All you've got to do now's to be 'pure and peaceable, gentle, easy to be entreated, and without hypocrisy.' That's about all there is to the Shaker creed, and that's enough to keep us all busy."

Sue ran in from the porch excitedly and caught her mother's hand.

"The cows have all gone into the barn," she chattered; "and the Shaker gentlemen are milking them, and not one of them is shaking the least bit, for I 'specially noticed; and I looked in through the porch window, and there is nice supper on a table—bread and butter and milk and dried-apple sauce and gingerbread and cottage cheese. Is it for us, Mardie?"

Susanna's lip was trembling and her face was pale. She lifted her swimming eyes to the Sister's and asked, "Is it for us, Eldress Abby?"

"Yee, it's for you," she answered; "there's always a Shaker supper on the table for all who want to leave the husks and share the feast. Come right in and help yourselves. I will sit down with you."

Supper was over, and Susanna and Sue were lying in a little upper chamber under the stars. It was the very one that Susanna had slept in as a child, or that she had been put to bed in, for there was little sleep that night for any one. She had leaned on the window-sill with her mother and watched the pillar of flame and smoke ascend from the burning barn; and once in the early morning she had stolen out of bed, and, kneeling by the open window, had watched the two silent Shaker brothers who were guarding the smoldering ruins, fearful lest the wind should rise and bear any spark to the roofs of the precious buildings they had labored so hard to save.

The chamber was spotless and devoid of ornament. The paint was robin's egg blue and of a satin gloss. The shining floor was of the same color, and neat braided rugs covered exposed places near the bureau, washstand, and bed. Various useful articles of Shaker manufacture interested Sue greatly: the exquisite straw-work that covered the whisk-broom; the mending-basket, pincushion, needle-book, spool and watch cases, hair-receivers, pin-trays, might all have been put together by fairy fingers.

Sue's prayers had been fervent, but a trifle disjointed, covering all subjects from Jack and Fardie, to Grandma in heaven and Aunt Louisa at the farm, with special references to El-der-ess Abby and the Shaker cows, and petitions that the next day be fair so that she could see them milked. Excitement at her strange, unaccustomed surroundings had put the child's mind in a very whirl, and she had astonished her mother with a very new and disturbing version of the Lord's prayer, ending: "God give us our debts and help us to forget our debtors and theirs shall be the glory, Amen." Now she lay quietly on the wall side of the clean, narrow bed, while her mother listened to hear the regular breathing that would mean that she was off for the land of dreams. The child's sleep would leave the mother free to slip out of bed and look at the stars; free to pray and long and wonder and suffer and repent,—not wholly, but in part, for she was really at peace in all but the innermost citadel of her conscience. She had left her husband, and for the moment, at all events, she was fiercely glad; but she had left her boy, and Jack was only ten. Jack was not the helpless, clinging sort; he was a little piece of his father, and his favorite. Aunt Louisa would surely take him, and Jack would scarcely feel the difference, for he had never shown any special affection for anybody. Still he was her child, nobody could possibly get around that fact, and it was a stumbling-block in the way of forgetfulness or ease of mind. Oh, but for that, what unspeakable content she could feel in this quiet haven, this self-respecting solitude! To have her thoughts, her emotions, her words, her *self*, to herself once more, as she had had them before she was married at seventeen. To go to sleep in peace, without listening for a step she had once heard with gladness, but that now sometimes stumbled unsteadily on the stair; or to dream as happy women dreamed, without being roused by the voice of the present John, a voice so different from that of the past John that it made the heart ache to listen to it.

Sue's voice broke the stillness: "How long are we going to stay here, Mardie?"

"I don't know, Sue; I think perhaps as long as they'll let us."

"Will Fardie come and see us?"

"I don't expect him."

"Who'll take care of Jack, Mardie?"

"Your Aunt Louisa."

"She'll scold him awfully, but he never cries; he just says, 'Pooh! what do I care?' Oh, I forgot to pray for that very nicest Shaker gentleman that said he'd let me help him feed the calves! Hadn't I better get out of bed and do it? I'd 'specially like to."

"Very well, Sue; and then go to sleep."

Safely in bed again, there was a long pause, and then the eager little voice began, "Who'll take care of Fardie now?"

"He's a big man; he doesn't need anybody."

"What if he's sick?"

"We must go back to him, I suppose."

"To-morrow's Sunday; what if he needs us to-morrow, Mardie?"

"I don't know, I don't know! Oh, Sue, Sue, don't ask your wretched mother any more questions, for she cannot bear them to-night. Cuddle up close to her; love her and forgive her and help her to know what's right."

"Yea" is always thus pronounced by the Shakers.

II

WHEN Susanna Nelson at seventeen married John Hathaway, she had the usual cogent reasons for so doing, with some rather more unusual ones added thereto. She was alone in the world, and her life with an uncle, her mother's only relative, was an unhappy one. No assistance in the household tasks that she had ever been able to render made her a welcome member of the family or kept her from feeling a burden, and she belonged no more to the little circle at seventeen, than she did when she became a part of it at twelve. The hope of being independent and earning her own living had sustained her through the last year; but it was a very timid, self-distrustful, love-starved little heart that John Hathaway stormed and carried by assault. Her girl's life in a country school and her uncle's very rigid and orthodox home had been devoid of emotion or experience; still, her mother had early sown seeds in her mind and spirit that even in the most arid soil were certain to flower into beauty when the time for flowering came; and intellectually Susanna was the clever daughter of clever parents. She was very immature, because, after early childhood, her environment had not been favorable to her development. At seventeen she began to dream of a future as bright as the past had been dreary and uneventful. Visions of happiness, of goodness, and of service haunted her, and sometimes, gleaming through the mists of dawning womanhood, the figure, all luminous, of The Man!

When John Hathaway appeared on the horizon, she promptly clothed him in all the beautiful garments of her dreams; they were a grotesque misfit, but when we intimate that women have confused the dream and the reality before, and may even do so again, we make the only possible excuse for poor little Susanna Nelson.

John Hathaway was the very image of the outer world that lay beyond Susanna's village. He was a fairly prosperous, genial, handsome young merchant, who looked upon life as a place furnished by Providence in which to have "a good time." His parents had frequently told him that it was expedient for him to "settle down," and he supposed that he might finally do so, if he should ever find a girl who would tempt him to relinquish his liberty. (The line that divides liberty and license was a little vague to John Hathaway!) It is curious that he should not have chosen for his life-partner some thoughtless, rosy, romping young person, whose highest conception of connubial happiness would have been to drive twenty miles to the seashore on a Sunday, and having partaken of all the season's delicacies, solid and liquid, to come home hilarious by moonlight. That, however, is not the way the little love-imps do their work in the world; or is it possible that they are not imps at all who provoke and stimulate and arrange these strange marriages—not imps, but honest, chastening little character-builders? In any event, the moment that John Hathaway first beheld Susanna Nelson was the moment of his surrender; yet the wooing was as incomprehensible as that of a fragile, dainty little hummingbird by a pompous, greedy, big-breasted robin.

Susanna was like a New England anemone. Her face was oval in shape and as smooth and pale as a pearl. Her hair was dark, not very heavy, and as soft as a child's. Her lips were delicate and sensitive, her eyes a cool gray,—clear, steady, and shaded by darker lashes. When John Hathaway met her shy, maidenly glance and heard her pretty, dovelike voice, it is strange he did not see that there was a bit too much saint in her to make her a willing comrade of his gay, roistering life. But as a matter of fact, John Hathaway saw nothing at all; nothing but that Susanna Nelson was a lovely girl and he wanted her for his own. The type was one he had never met before, one that allured him by its mysteries and piqued him by its shy aloofness.

John had a "way with him,"—a way that speedily won Susanna; and after all there was a best to him as well as a worst. He had a twinkling eye, an infectious laugh, a sweet disposition, and while he was over-susceptible to the charm of a pretty face, he had a chivalrous admiration for all women, coupled, it must be confessed, with a decided lack of discrimination in values. His boyish light-heartedness had a charm for everybody, including Susanna; a charm that lasted until she discovered that his heart was light not only when it ought to be light, but when it ought to be heavy.

He was very much in love with her, but there was nothing particularly exclusive, unique, individual, or interesting about his passion at that time. It was of the every-day sort which carries a well-meaning man to the altar, and sometimes, in cases of exceptional fervor and duration, even a little farther. Stock sizes of this article are common and inexpensive, and John Hathaway's love when he married Susanna was, judged by the highest standards, about as trivial an affair as Cupid ever put upon the market or a man ever offered to a woman. Susanna on the same day offered John, or the wooden idol she was worshiping as John, her whole self—mind, body, heart, and spirit. So the couple were united, and smilingly signed the marriage-register, a rite by which their love for each other was supposed to be made eternal.

"Will you love me?" said he."Will you love me?" said she.Then they answered together:—"Through foul and fair weather,From sunrise to moonrise,From moonrise to sunrise,By heath and by harbour,In orchard or arbour,In the time of the rose,In the time of the snows,Through smoke and through smotherWe'll love one another!"

Cinderella, when the lover-prince discovers her and fits the crystal slipper to her foot, makes short work of flinging away her rags; and in some such pretty, airy, unthinking way did Susanna fling aside the dullness, inhospitality, and ugliness of her uncle's home and depart in a cloud of glory on her wedding journey. She had been lonely, now she would have companionship. She had been of no consequence, now she would be queen of her own small domain. She had been last with everybody, now she would be first with one, at least. She had worked hard and received neither compensation nor gratitude; henceforward her service would be gladly rendered at an altar where votive offerings would not be taken as a matter of course. She was only a slip of a girl now; marriage and housewifely cares would make her a woman. Some time perhaps the last great experience of life would come to her, and then what a crown of joys would be hers,—love, husband, home, children! What a vision it was, and how soon the chief glory of it faded!

Never were two beings more hopelessly unlike than John Hathaway single and John Hathaway married, but the bliss lasted a few years, nevertheless: partly because Susanna's charm was deep and penetrating, the sort to hold a false man for a time and a true man forever; partly because she tried, as a girl or woman has seldom tried before, to do her duty and to keep her own ideal unshattered.

John had always been convivial, but Susanna at seventeen had been at once too innocent and too ignorant to judge a man's tendencies truly, or to rate his character at its real worth. As time went on, his earlier leanings grew more definite; he spent on pleasure far more than he could afford, and his conduct became a byword in the neighborhood. His boy he loved. He felt on a level with Jack, could understand him, play with him, punish him, and make friends with him; but little Sue was different. She always seemed to him the concentrated essence of her mother's soul, and when unhappy days came, he never looked in her radiant, searching eyes without a consciousness of inferiority. The little creature had loved her jolly, handsome, careless father at first, even though she feared him; but of late she had grown shy, silent, and timid, for his indifference chilled her and she flung herself upon her mother's love with an almost unchildlike intensity. This unhappy relation between the child and the father gave Susanna's heart new pangs. She still loved her husband,—not dearly, but a good deal; and over and above that remnant of the old love which still endured she gave him unstinted care and hopeful maternal tenderness.

The crash came in course of time. John transcended the bounds of his wife's patience more and more. She made her last protests; then she took one passionate day to make up her mind,—a day when John and the boy were away together; a day of complete revolt against everything she was facing in the present, and, so far as she could see, everything that she had to face in the future. Prayer for light left her in darkness, and she had no human creature to advise her. Conscience was overthrown; she could see no duty save to her own outraged personality. Often and often during the year just past she had thought of the peace, the grateful solitude and shelter of that Shaker Settlement hidden among New England orchards; that quiet haven where there was neither marrying nor giving in marriage. Now her bruised heart longed for such a life of nun-like simplicity and consecration, wheremen and women met only as brothers and sisters, where they worked side by side with no thought of personal passion or personal gain, but only for the common good of the community.

Albion village was less than three hours distant by train. She hastily gathered her plainest clothes and Sue's, packed them in a small trunk, took her mother's watch, her own little store of money and the twenty-dollar gold piece John's senior partner had given Sue on her last birthday, wrote a letter of good-by to John, and went out of her cottage gate in a storm of feeling so tumultuous that there was no room for reflection. Besides, she had reflected, and reflected, for months and months, so she would have said, and the time had come for action. Susanna was not unlettered, but she certainly had never read Meredith or she would have learned that "love is an affair of two, and only for two that can be as quick, as constant in intercommunication as are sun and earth, through the cloud, or face to face. They take their breath of life from each other in signs of affection, proofs of faithfulness, incentives to admiration. But a solitary soul dragging a log must make the log a God to rejoice in the burden." The demigod that poor, blind Susanna married had vanished, and she could drag the log no longer, but she made one mistake in judging her husband, in that she regarded him, at thirty-two, as a finished product, a man who was finally this and that, and behaved thus and so, and would never be any different.

The "age of discretion" is a movable feast of extraordinary uncertainty, and John Hathaway was a little behindhand in overtaking it. As a matter of fact, he had never for an instant looked life squarely in the face. He took a casual glance at it now and then, after he was married, but it presented no very distinguishable features, nothing to make him stop and think, nothing to arouse in him any special sense of responsibility. Boys have a way of "growing up," however, sooner or later, at least most of them have, and that possibility was not sufficiently in the foreground of Susanna's mind when she finished what she considered an exhaustive study of her husband's character.

"I am leaving you, John [she wrote], to see if I can keep the little love I have left for you as the father of my children. I seem to have lost all the rest of it living with you. I am not perfectly sure that I am right in going, for everybody seems to think that women, mothers especially, should bear anything rather than desert the home. I could not take Jack away, for you love him and he will be a comfort to you. A comfort to you, yes, but what will you be to him now that he is growing older? That is the thought that troubles me, yet I dare not take him with me when he is half yours. You will not miss me, nor will the loss of Sue make any difference. Oh, John! how can you help loving that blessed little creature, so much better and so much more gifted than either of us that we can only wonder how we came to be her father and mother? Your sin against her is greater than that against me, for at least you are not responsible for bringing *me* into the world. I know Louisa will take care of Jack, and she lives so near that you can see him as often as you wish. I shall let her know my address, which I have asked her to keep to herself. She will write to me if you or Jack should be seriously ill, but not for any other reason.

"As for you, there is nothing more that I can say except to confess freely that I was not the right wife for you and that mine was not the only mistake. I have tried my very best to meet you in everything that was not absolutely wrong, and I have used all the arguments I could think of, but it only made matters worse. I thought I knew you, John, in the old days. How comes it that we have traveled so far apart, we who began together? It seems to me that some time you must come to your senses and take up your life seriously, for this is not life, the sorry thing you have lived lately, but I cannot wait any longer! I am tired, tired, tired of waiting and hoping, too tired to do anything but drag myself away from the sight of your folly. You have wasted our children's substance, indulged your appetites until you have lost the respect of your best friends, and you have made me—who was your choice, your wife, the head of your house, the woman who brought your children into the world—you have made me an object of pity; a poor, neglected thing who could not meet her neighbors' eyes without blushing."

When Jack and his father returned from their outing at eight o'clock in the evening, having had supper at a wayside hotel, the boy went to bed philosophically, lighting his lamp for himself, the conclusion being that the two other members of the household were a little late, but would be in presently.

The next morning was bright and fair. Jack waked at cockcrow, and after calling to his mother and Sue, jumped out of bed, ran into their rooms to find them empty, then bounced down the stairs two at a time, going through the sitting-room on his way to find Ellen in the kitchen. His father was sitting at the table with the still-lighted student lamp on it; the table where lessons had been learned, books read, stories told, mending done, checkers and dominoes played; the big, round walnut table that was the focus of the family life—but mother's table, not father's.

John Hathaway had never left his chair nor taken off his hat. His cane leaned against his knee, his gloves were in his left hand, while the right held Susanna's letter.

He was asleep, although his lips twitched and he stirred uneasily. His face was haggard, and behind his closed lids, somewhere in the centre of thought and memory, a train of fiery words burned in an ever-widening circle, round and round and round, ploughing, searing their way through some obscure part of him that had heretofore been without feeling, but was now all quick and alive with sensation.

"You have made me—who was your choice, your wife, the head of your house, the woman who brought your children into the world—you have made me an object of pity; a poor, neglected thing who could not meet her neighbors' eyes without blushing."

Any one who wished to pierce John Hathaway's armor at that period of his life would have had to use a very sharp and pointed arrow, for he was well wadded with the belief that a man has a right to do what he likes. Susanna's shaft was tipped with truth and dipped in the blood of her outraged heart. The stored-up force of silent years went into the speeding of it. She had never shot an arrow before, and her skill was instinctive rather than scientific, but the powers were on her side and she aimed better than she knew—those who took note of John Hathaway's behavior that summer would have testified willingly to that. It was the summer in which his boyish irresponsibility slipped away from him once and for all; a summer in which the face of life ceased to be an indistinguishable mass of meaningless events and disclosed an order, a reason, a purpose hitherto unseen and undefined. The boy "grew up," rather tardily it must be confessed. His soul had not added a cubit to its stature in sunshine, gayety, and prosperity; it took the shock of grief, hurt pride, solitude, and remorse to make a man of John Hathaway.

III

IT was a radiant July morning in Albion village, and when Sue first beheld it from the bedroom window at the Shaker Settlement, she had wished ardently that it might never, never grow dark, and that Jack and Fardie might be having the very same sunshine in Farnham. It was not noon yet, but experience had in some way tempered the completeness of her joy, for the marks of tears were on her pretty little face. She had neither been scolded nor punished, but she had been dragged away from a delicious play without any adequate reason. She had disappeared after breakfast, while Susanna was helping Sister Tabitha with the beds and the dishes, but as she was the most docile of children, her mother never thought of anxiety. At nine o'clock Eldress Abby took Susanna to the laundry house, and there under a spreading maple were Sue and the two youngest little Shakeresses, children of seven and eight respectively. Sue was directing the plays: chattering, planning, ordering, and suggesting expedients to her slower-minded and less-experienced companions. They had dragged a large box from one of the sheds and set it up under the tree. The interior had been quickly converted into a commodious residence, one not in the least of a Shaker type. Small bluing-boxes served for bedstead and dining-table, bits of broken china for the dishes, while tiny flat stones were the seats, and four clothes-pins, tastefully clad in handkerchiefs, surrounded the table.

"Do they kneel in prayer before they eat, as all Believers do?" asked Shaker Mary.

"I don't believe Adam and Eve was Believers, 'cause who would have taught them to be?" replied Sue; "still we might let them pray, anyway, though clothes-pins don't kneel nicely."

"I've got another one all dressed," said little Shaker Jane.

"We can't have any more; Adam and Eve didn't have only two children in my Sunday-school lesson,—Cain and Abel," objected Sue.

"Can't this one be a company?" pleaded Mary, anxious not to waste the clothes-pin.

"But where could comp'ny come from?" queried Sue. "There wasn't any more people anywheres but just Adam and Eve and Cain and Abel. Put the clothes-pin in your apron-pocket, Jane, and bimeby we'll let Eve have a little new baby, and I'll get Mardie to name it right out of the Bible. Now let's begin. Adam is awfully tired this morning; he says, 'Eve, I've been workin' all night and I can't eat my breakfuss.' Now, Mary, you be Cain, he's alittle boy, and you must say, 'Fardie, play a little with me, please!' and Fardie will say, 'Child'en shouldn't talk at the—'"

What subjects of conversation would have been aired at the Adamic family board before breakfast was finished will never be known, for Eldress Abby, with a firm but not unkind grasp, took Shaker Jane and Mary by their little hands and said, "Morning's not the time for play; run over to Sister Martha and help her shell the peas; then there'll be your seams to oversew."

Sue watched the disappearing children and saw the fabric of her dream fade into thin air; but she was a person of considerable individuality for her years. Her lip quivered, tears rushed to her eyes and flowed silently down her cheeks, but without a glance at Eldress Abby or a word of comment she walked slowly away from the laundry, her chin high.

"Sue meant all right, she was only playing the plays of the world," said Eldress Abby, "but you can well understand, Susanna, that we can't let our Shaker children play that way and get wrong ideas into their heads at the beginning. We don't condemn an honest, orderly marriage as a worldly institution, but we claim it has no place in Christ's kingdom; therefore we leave it to the world, where it belongs. The world's people live on the lower plane of Adam; the Shakers try to live on the Christ plane, in virgin purity, long-suffering, meekness, and patience."

"I see, I know," Susanna answered slowly, with a little glance at injured Sue walking toward the house, "but we needn't leave the children unhappy this morning, for I can think of a play that will comfort them and please you.— Come back, Sue! Wait a minute, Mary and Jane, before you go to Sister Martha! We will play the story that Sister Tabitha told us last week. Do you remember about Mother Ann Lee in the English prison? The soap-box will be her cell, for it was so small she could not lie down in it. Take some of the shingles, Jane, and close up the open side of the box. Do you see the large brown spot in one of them, Mary? Push that very hard with a clothes-pin and there'll be a hole through the shingle;—that's right! Now, Sister Tabitha said that Mother Ann was kept for days without food, for people thought she was a wicked, dangerous woman, and they would have been willing to let her die of starvation. But there was a great key-hole in the door, and James Whittaker, a boy of nineteen, who loved Mother Ann and believed in her, put the stem of a clay pipe in the hole and poured a mixture of wine and milk through it. He managed to do this day after day, so that when the jailer opened the cell door, expecting to find Mother Ann dying for lack of food, she walked out looking almost as strong and well as when she entered. You can play it all out, and afterwards you can make the ship that brought Mother Ann and the other Shakers from Liverpool to New York. The clothes-pins can be—who will they be, Jane?"

"William Lee, Nancy Lee, James Whittaker, and I forget the others," recited Jane, like an obedient parrot.

"And it will be splendid to have James Whittaker, for he really came to Albion," said Mary.

"Perhaps he stood on this very spot more than once," mused Abby. "It was Mother Ann's vision that brought them to this land,—a vision of a large tree with outstretching branches, every leaf of which shone with the brightness of a burning torch! Oh! if the vision would only come true! If Believers would only come to us as many as the leaves on the tree," she sighed, as she and Susanna moved away from the group of chattering children, all as eager to play the history of Shakerism as they had been to dramatize the family life of Adam and Eve.

"There must be so many men and women without ties, living useless lives, with no aim or object in them," Susanna said, "I wonder that more of them do not find their way here. The peace and goodness and helpfulness of the life sink straight into my heart. The Brothers and Sisters are so friendly and cheery with one another; there is neither gossip nor hard words; there is pleasant work, and your thoughts seem to be all so concentrated upon right living that it is like heaven below, only I feel that the cross is there, bravely as you all bear it."

"There are roses on my cross most beautiful to see,As I turn from all the dross from which it sets me free,"
quoted Eldress Abby, devoutly.

"It is easy enough for me," continued Susanna, "for it was no cross for me to give up my husband at the time; but oh, if a woman had a considerate, loving man to live with, one who would strengthen her and help her to be good, one who would protect and cherish her, one who would be an example to his children and bring them up in the fear of the Lord—that would be heaven below, too; and how could she bear to give it all up when it seems so good, so true, so right? Mightn't two people walk together to God if both chose the same path?"

"It's my belief that one can find the road better alone than when somebody else is going alongside to distract them. Not that the Lord is going to turn anybody away, not even when they bring Him a lot of burned-out trash for a gift," said Eldress Abby, bluntly. "But don't you believe He sees the difference between a person that comes to Him when there is nowhere else to turn—a person that's tried all and found it wanting—and one that gives up freely pleasure, and gain, and husband, and home, to follow the Christ life?"

"Yes, He must, He must," Susanna answered faintly. "But the children, Eldress Abby! If you hadn't any, you could perhaps keep yourself from wanting them; but if you had, how could you give them up? Jesus was the great Saviour of mankind, but next to Him it seems as if the children had been the little saviours, from the time the first one was born until this very day!"

"Yee, I've no doubt they keep the worst of the world's people, those that are living in carnal marriage without a thought of godliness,—I've no doubt children keep that sort from going to the lowest perdition," allowed Eldress Abby; "and those we bring up in the Community make the best converts; but to a Shaker, the greater the sacrifice, the greater the glory. I wish you was gathered in, Susanna, for your hands and feet are quick to serve, your face is turned toward the truth, and your heart is all ready to receive the revelation."

"I wish I needn't turn my back on one set of duties to take up another," murmured Susanna, timidly.

"Yee; no doubt you do. Your business is to find out which are the higher duties, and then do *those*. Just make up your mind whether you'd rather replenish earth, as you've been doing, or replenish heaven, as we're trying to do.—But I must go to my work; ten o'clock in the morning's a poor time to be discussing doctrine! You're for weeding, Susanna, I suppose?"

Brother Ansel was seated at a grindstone under the apple trees, teaching (intermittently) a couple of boys to grind a scythe, when Susanna came to her work in the herb-garden, Sue walking discreetly at her heels.

Ansel was a slow-moving, humorously-inclined, easy-going Brother, who was drifting into the kingdom of heaven without any special effort on his part.

"I'd 'bout as lives be a Shaker as anything else," had been his rather dubious statement of faith when he requested admittance into the band of Believers. "No more crosses, accordin' to my notion, an' consid'able more chance o' crowns!"

His experience of life "on the Adamic plane," the holy estate of matrimony, being the chief sin of this way of thought, had disposed him to regard woman as an apparently necessary, but not especially desirable, being. The theory of holding property in common had no terrors for him. He was generous, unambitious, frugal-minded, somewhat lacking in energy, and just as actively interested in his brother's welfare as in his own, which is perhaps not saying much. Shakerism was to him not a craving of the spirit, not a longing of the soul, but a simple, prudent theory of existence, lessening the various risks that man is exposed to in his journey through this vale of tears.

"Women-folks makes splendid Shakers," he was wont to say. "They're all right as Sisters, 'cause their belief makes 'em safe. It kind o' shears 'em o' their strength; tames their sperits; takes the sting out of 'em an' keeps 'em from bein' sassy an' domineerin'. Jest as long as they think marriage is*right*, they'll marry ye spite of anything ye can do or say—four of 'em married my father one after another, though he fit 'em off as hard as he knew how. But if ye can once get the faith o' Mother Ann into 'em, they're as good afterwards as they was wicked afore. There's no stoppin' women-folks once ye get 'em started; they don't keer whether it's heaven or the other place, so long as they get where they want to go!"

Elder Daniel Gray had heard Brother Ansel state his religious theories more than once when he was first "gathered in," and secretly lamented the lack of spirituality in the new convert. The Elder was an instrument more finely attuned; sober, humble, pure-minded, zealous, consecrated to the truth as he saw it, he labored in and out of season for the faith he held so dear; yet as the years went on, he noted that Ansel, notwithstanding his eccentric views, lived an honest, temperate, God-fearing life, talking no scandal, dwelling in unity with his brethren and sisters, and upholding the banner of Shakerism in his own peculiar way.

As Susanna approached him, Ansel called out, "The yairbs are all ready for ye, Susanna; the weeds have been on the rampage sence yesterday's rain. Seems like the more uselesser a thing is, the more it flourishes. The yairbs grow; oh, yes, they make out to *grow*; but you don't see 'em come leapin' an' tearin' out o' the airth like weeds. Then there's the birds! I've jest been stoppin' my grindin' to look at 'em carry on. Take 'em all in all, there ain'tnothin' so lazy an' aimless an' busy'boutnothin' as birds. They go kitin' 'roun' from tree to tree, hoppin' an' chirpin', flyin' here an' there 'thout no airthlyobjeck 'ceptin' to fly back ag'in. There's a heap o' useless critters in the univarse, but I guess birds are 'bout the uselyest, 'less it's grasshoppers, mebbe."

"I don't care what you say about the grasshoppers, Ansel, but you shan't abuse the birds," said Susanna, stooping over the beds of tansy and sage, thyme and summer savory. "Weeds or no weeds, we're going to have a great crop of herbs this year, Ansel!"

"Yee, so we be! We sowed more'n usual so's to keep the two 'jiners' at work long's we could.—Take that scythe over to the barn, Jacob, an' fetch me another, an' step spry."

"What's a jiner, Ansel?"

"Winter Shakers, I call 'em. They're reg'larconstitooshanal dyed-in-the-wool jiners, jinin' most anything an' hookin' on most anywheres. They jine when it comes on too cold to sleep outdoors, an' they onjine when it comes on spring. Elder Gray's always hopin' to gather in new souls, so he gives the best of 'em a few months' trial. How are ye, Hannah?" he called to a Sister passing through the orchard to search for any possible green apples under the trees. "Make us a good old-fashioned deep-dish pandowdy an' we'll all do our best to eat it!"

"I suppose the 'jiners' get discouraged and fear they can't keep up to the standard. Not everybody is good enough to lead a self-denying Shaker life," said Susanna, pushing back the close sunbonnet from her warm face, which had grown younger, smoother, and sweeter in the last few weeks.

"Nay, I s'pose likely; 'less they're same as me, a born Shaker," Ansel replied. "I don't hanker after strong drink; don't like tobaccer (always could keep my temper 'thoutsmokin'), ain'tpartic'lar 'bout meat-eatin', don't keer 'bout heapin' up riches, can't 'stand the ways o' worldly women-folks, jest as lives confess my sins to the Elder as not, 'cause I hain't sinned any to amount to anything sence I made my first confession; there I be, a natural follerer o' Mother Ann Lee."

Susanna drew her Shaker bonnet forward over her eyes and turned her back to Brother Ansel under the pretense of reaching over to the rows of sweet marjoram. She had never supposed it possible that she could laugh again, and indeed she seldom felt like it, but Ansel's interpretations of Shaker doctrine were almost too much for her latent sense of humor.

"What *are* you smiling at, and me so sad, Mardie?" quavered Sue, piteously, from the little plot of easy weeding her mother had given her to do. "I keep remembering my game! It was such a *Christian* game, too. Lots nicer than Mother Ann in prison; for Jane said her mother and father was both Believers, and nobody was good enough to pour milk through the key-hole but her. I wanted to give the clothes-pins story names, like Hilda and Percy, but I called them Adam and Eve and Cain and Abel just because I thought the Shakers would 'specially like a Bible play. I love Elderess Abby, but she does stop my happiness, Mardie. That's the second time to-day, for she took Moses away from me when I was kissing him because he pinched his thumb in the window."

"Why did you do that, Sue?" remonstrated her mother softly, remembering Ansel's proximity. "You never used to kiss strange little boys at home in Farnham."

"Moses isn't a boy; he's only six, and that's a baby; besides, I like him better than any little boys at home, and that's the reason I kissed him; there's no harm in boy-kissing, is there, Mardie?"

"You don't know anybody here very well yet; not well enough to kiss them," Susanna answered, rather hopeless as to the best way of inculcating the undesirability of the Adamic plane of thought at this early age. "While we stay here, Sue, we ought both to be very careful to do exactly as the Shakers do."

By this time mother and child had reached the orchard end of a row, and Brother Ansel was thirstily waiting to deliver a little more of the information with which his mind was always teeming.

"Them Boston people that come over to our public meetin' last Sunday," he began, "they was dretfulscairt 'bout what would become o' the human race if it should all turn Shakers. 'I guess you needn't worry,' I says; 'it'll take consid'able of a spell to convert all you city folks,' I says, 'an' after all, what if the world should come to an end?' I says. 'If half we hear is true 'bout the way folks carry on in New York and Chicago, it's 'bout time it stopped,' I says, 'an' I guess the Lord could do a consid'able better job on a second one,' I says, 'after findin' out the weak places in this.' They can't stand givin' up their possessions, the world's folks; that's the principal trouble with 'em! If you don't have nothin' to give up,—like some o' the tramps that happen along here and convince the Elder they're jest bustin' with the fear o' God,—why, o' course 't ain't no trick at all to be a Believer."

"Did you have much to give up, Brother Ansel?" Susanna asked.

"'Bout's much as any sinner ever had that jined this Community," replied Ansel, complacently. "The list o' what I consecrated to this Society when I was gathered in was: One horse, one wagon, one two-year-old heifer, one axe, one saddle, one padlock, one bed and bedding, four turkeys, eleven hens, one pair o' plough-irons, two chains, and eleven dollars in cash.—Can you beat that?"

"Oh, yes, *things*!" said Susanna, absent-mindedly. "I was thinking of family and friends, pleasures and memories and ambitions and hopes."

"I guess it don't pinch you any worse to give up a hope than it would a good two-year-old heifer," retorted Ansel; "but there, you can't never tell what folks'll hang on to the hardest! The man that drove them Boston folks over here last Sunday,—did you notice him? the one that had the sister with a bright red dress an' hat on?—Land! I could think just how hell must look whenever my eye lighted on that girl's git-up!—Well, I done my best to exhort that driver, bein' as how we had a good chance to talk while we was hitchin' an' unhitchin' the team; an' Elder Gray always says I ain't earnest enough in preachin' the faith;—but he didn't learn anything from the meetin'. Kep' his eye on the Shaker bunnits, an' took notice o' the marchin' an' dancin', but he didn't care nothin' 'bout doctrine.

"'I draw the line at bein' a cerebrate,' he says. 'I'm willin' to sell all my goods an' divide with the poor,' he says, 'but I ain'tgoin' to be no cerebrate. If I don't have no other luxuries, I will have a wife,' he says. 'I've hed three, an' if this one don't last me out, I'll get another, if it's only to start the kitchen fire in the mornin' an' put the cat in the shed nights!'"

IV

Louisa otherwise Mrs. Adlai Banks, the elder sister of Susanna's husband, was a rock-ribbed widow of forty-five summers,—forty-five winters would seem a better phrase in which to assert her age,—who resided on a small farm twenty miles from the manufacturing town of Farnham.

When the Fates were bestowing qualities of mind and heart upon the Hathaway babies, they gave the more graceful, genial, likable ones to John,—not realizing, perhaps, what bad use he would make of them,—and endowed Louisa with great deposits of honesty, sincerity, energy, piety, and frugality, all so mysteriously compounded that they turned to granite in her hands. If she had been consulted, it would have been all the same. She would never have accepted John's charm of personality at the expense of being saddled with his weaknesses, and he would not have taken her cast-iron virtues at any price whatsoever.

She was sweeping her porch on that day in May when Susanna and Sue had wakened in the bare upper chamber at the Shaker Settlement—Sue clear-eyed, jubilant, expectant, unafraid; Susanna pale from her fitful sleep, weary with the burden of her heart.

Looking down the road, Mrs. Banks espied the form of her brother John walking in her direction and leading Jack by the hand.

This was a most unusual sight, for John's calls had been uncommonly few of late years, since a man rarely visits a lady relative for the mere purpose of hearing "a piece of her mind." This piece, large, solid, highly flavored with pepper, and as acid as mental vinegar could make it, was Louisa Banks's only contribution to conversation when she met her brother. She could not stop for any airy persiflage about weather, crops, or politics when her one desire was to tell him what she thought of him.

"Good-morning, Louisa. Shake hands with your aunt, Jack."

"He can't till I'm through sweeping. Good-morning, John; what brings you here?"

John sat down on the steps, and Jack flew to the barn, where there was generally an amiable hired man and a cheerful cow, both infinitely better company than his highly respected and wealthy aunt.

"I came because I had to bring the boy to the only relation I've got in the world," John answered tersely. "My wife's left me."

"Well, she's been a great while doing it," remarked Louisa, digging her broom into the cracks of the piazza floor and making no pause for reflection. "If she hadn't had the patience of Job and the meekness of Moses, she'd have gone long before. Where'd she go?"

"I don't know; she didn't say."

"Did you take the trouble to look through the house for her? I ain't certain you fairly know her by sight nowadays, do you?"

John flushed crimson, but bit his lip in an attempt to keep his temper. "She left a letter," he said, "and she took Sue with her."

"That was all right; Sue's a nervous little thing and needs at least one parent; she hasn't been used to more, so she won't miss anything. Jack's like most of the Hathaways; he'll grow up his own way, without anybody's help or hindrance. What are you going to do with him?"

"Leave him with you, of course. What else could I do?"

"Very well, I'll take him, and while I'm about it I'd like to give you a piece of my mind."

John was fighting for self-control, but he was too wretched and remorseful for rage to have any real sway over him.

"Is it the same old piece, or a different one?" he asked, setting his teeth grimly. "I shouldn't think you'd have any mind left, you've given so many pieces of it to me already."

"I have some left, and plenty, too," answered Louisa, dashing into the house, banging the broom into a corner, coming out again like a breeze, and slamming the door behind her. "You can leave the boy here and welcome; I'll take good care of him, and if you don't send me twenty dollars a month for his food and clothes, I'll turn him outdoors. The more responsibility other folks rid you of, the more you'll let 'em, and I won't take a feather's weight off you for fear you'll sink into everlasting perdition."

"I didn't expect any sympathy from you," said John, drearily, pulling himself up from the steps and leaning against the honeysuckle trellis. "Susanna's just the same. Women are all as hard as the nether millstone. They're hard if they're angels, and hard if they're devils; it doesn't make much difference."

"I guess you've found a few soft ones, if report says true," returned Louisa, bluntly. "You'd better go and get some of their sympathy, the kind you can buy and pay for. The way you've ruined your life turns me fairly sick. You had a good father and mother, good education and advantages, enough money to start you in business, the best of wives, and two children any man could be proud of, one of 'em especially. You've thrown 'em all away, and what for? Horses and cards and gay company, late suppers, with wine, and for aught I know, whiskey,—you the son of a man who didn't know the taste of ginger beer! You've spent your days and nights with a pack of carousing men and women that would take your last cent and not leave you enough for honest burial."

"It's a pity we didn't make a traveling preacher of you!" exclaimed John, bitterly. "Lord Almighty, I wonder how such women as you can live in the world, you know so little about it, and so little about men."

"I know all I want to about 'em," retorted Louisa, "and precious little that's good. They're a gluttonous, self-indulgent, extravagant, reckless, pleasure-loving lot! My husband was one of the best of 'em, and he wouldn't have amounted to a hill of beans if I hadn't devoted fifteen years to disciplining, uplifting, and strengthening him!"

"You managed to strengthen him so that he died before he was fifty!"

"It don't matter when a man dies," said the remorseless Mrs. Banks, "if he's succeeded in living a decent, God-fearing life. As for you, John Hathaway, I'll tell you the truth if you are my brother, for Susanna's too much of a saint to speak out."

"Don't be afraid; Susanna's spoken out at last, plainly enough to please even you!"

"I'm glad of it, for I didn't suppose she had spunk enough to resent anything. I shall be sorry to-morrow, 's likely as not, for freeing my mind as much as I have, but my temper's up and I'm going to be the humble instrument of Providence and try to turn you from the error of your ways. You've defaced and degraded the temple the Lord built for you, and if He should come this minute and try to turn out the crowd of evil-doers you've kept in it, I doubt if He could!"

"I hope He'll approve of the way you've used your 'temple,'" said John, with stinging emphasis. "I shouldn't want to live in such a noisy one myself; I'd rather be a bat in a belfry. Good-by; I've had a pleasant call, as usual, and you've been a real sister to me in my trouble. You shall have the twenty dollars a month. Jack's clothes are in that valise, and there'll be a trunk to-morrow. Susanna said she'd write and let you know her whereabouts."

So saying, John Hathaway strode down the path, closed the gate behind him, and walked rapidly along the road that led to the station. It was a quiet road and he met few persons. He had neither dressed nor shaved since the day before; his face was haggard, his heart was like a lump of lead in his breast. Of what use to go to the empty house in Farnham when he could stifle his misery by a night with his friends?

No, he could not do that, either! The very thought of them brought a sense of satiety and disgust; the craving for what they would give him would come again in time, no doubt, but for the moment he was sick to the very soul of all they stood for. The feeling of complete helplessness, of desertion, of being alone in mid-ocean without a sail or a star in sight, mounted and swept over him. Susanna had been his sail, his star, although he had never fully realized it, and he had cut himself adrift from her pure, steadfast love, blinding himself with cheap and vulgar charms.

The next train to Farnham was not due for an hour. His steps faltered; he turned into a clump of trees by the wayside and flung himself on the ground to cry like a child, he who had not shed a tear since he was a boy of ten.

If Susanna could have seen that often longed-for burst of despair and remorse, that sudden recognition of his sins against himself and her, that gush of penitent tears, her heart might have softened once again; a flicker of flame might have lighted the ashes of her dying love; she might have taken his head on her shoulder, and said, "Never mind, John! Let's forget, and begin all over again!"

Matters did not look any brighter for John the next week, for his senior partner, Joel Atterbury, requested him to withdraw from the firm as soon as matters could be legally arranged. He was told that he had not been doing, nor earning, his share; that his way of living during the year just past had not been any credit to "the concern," and that he, Atterbury, sympathized too heartily with Mrs. John Hathaway to take any pleasure in doing business with Mr. John.

John's remnant of pride, completely humbled by this last withdrawal of confidence, would not suffer him to tell Atterbury that he had come to his senses and bidden farewell to the old life, or so he hoped and believed.

To lose a wife and child in a way infinitely worse than death; to hear the unwelcome truth that as a husband you have grown so offensive as to be beyond endurance; to have your own sister tell you that you richly deserve such treatment; to be virtually dismissed from a valuable business connection;—all this is enough to sober any man above the grade of a moral idiot, and John was not that; he was simply a self-indulgent, pleasure-loving, thoughtless, willful fellow, without any great amount of principle. He took his medicine, however, said nothing, and did his share of the business from day to day doggedly, keeping away from his partner as much as possible.

Ellen, the faithful maid of all work, stayed on with him at the old home; Jack wrote to him every week, and often came to spend Sunday with him.

"Aunt Louisa's real good to me," he told his father, "but she's not like mother. Seems to me mother's kind of selfish staying away from us so long. When do you expect her back?"

"I don't know; not before winter, I'm afraid; and don't call her selfish, I won't have it! Your mother never knew she had a self."

"If she'd only left Sue behind, we could have had more good times, we three together!"

"No, our family is four, Jack, and we can never have any good times, one, two, or three of us, because we're four! When one's away, whichever it is, it's wrong, but it's the worst when it's mother. Does your Aunt Louisa write to her?"

"Yes, sometimes, but she never lets me post the letters."

"Do you write to your mother? You ought to, you know, even if you don't have time for me. You could ask your aunt to enclose your letters in hers."

"Do you write to her, father?"

"Yes, I write twice a week," John answered, thinking drearily of the semi-weekly notes posted in Susanna's empty work-table upstairs. Would she ever read them? He doubted it, unless he died, and she came back to settle his affairs; but of course he shouldn't die,—no such good luck. Would a man die who breakfasted at eight, dined at one, supped at six, and went to bed at ten? Would a man die who worked in the garden an hour every afternoon, with half a day Saturday; that being the task most disagreeable to him and most appropriate therefore for penance?

Susanna loved flowers and had always wanted a garden, but John had been too much occupied with his own concerns to give her the needed help or money so that she could carry out her plans. The last year she had lost heart in many ways, so that little or nothing had been accomplished of all she had dreamed. It would have been laughable, had it not been pathetic, to see John Hathaway dig, delve, grub, sow, water, weed, transplant, generally at the wrong moment, in that dream-garden of Susanna's. He asked no advice and read no books. With feverish intensity, with complete ignorance of Nature's laws and small sympathy with their intricacies, he dug, hoed, raked, fertilized, and planted during that lonely summer. His absent-mindedness caused some expensive failures, as when the wide expanse of Susanna's drying ground, which was to be velvety lawn, "came up" curly lettuce; but he rooted out his frequent mistakes and patiently planted seeds or roots or bulbs over and over and over and over, until something sprouted in his beds, whether it was what he intended or not. While he weeded the brilliant orange nasturtiums, growing beside the magenta portulacca in a friendly proximity that certainly would never have existed had the mistress of the house been the head-gardener, he thought of nothing but his wife. He knew her pride, her reserve, her sensitive spirit; he knew her love of truth and honor and purity, the standards of life and conduct she had tried to hold him to so valiantly, and which he had so dragged in the dust during the blindness and the insanity of the last two years.

He, John Hathaway, was a deserted husband; Susanna had crept away all wounded and resentful. Where was she living and how supporting herself and Sue, when she could not have had a hundred dollars in the world? Probably Louisa was the source of income; conscientious, infernally disagreeable Louisa!

Would not the rumor of his changed habit of life reach her by some means in her place of hiding, sooner or later? Would she not yearn for a sight of Jack? Would she not finally give him a chance to ask forgiveness, or had she lost every trace of affection for him, as her letter seemed to imply? He walked the garden paths, with these and other unanswerable questions, and when he went to his lonely room at night, he held the lamp up to a bit of poetry that he had cut from a magazine and pinned to the looking-glass. If John Hathaway could be brought to the reading of poetry, he might even glance at the Bible in course of time, Louisa would have said. It was in May that Susanna had gone, and the first line of verse held his attention.

"May comes, day comes,One who was away comes;All the earth is glad
again,Kind and fair to me.

"May comes, day comes,One who was away comes;Set her place at hearth and
boardAs it used to be.

"May comes, day comes,One who was away comes;Higher are the hills of
home,Bluer is the sea."

The Hathaway house was in the suburbs, on a rise of ground, and as John
turned to the window he saw the full moon hanging yellow in the sky. It shone
on the verdant slopes and low wooded hills that surrounded the town, and cast
a glittering pathway on the ocean that bathed the beaches of the near-by shore.

"How long shall I have to wait," he wondered, "before my hills of home look
higher, and my sea bluer, because Susanna has come back to 'hearth and
board'!"

V

Susanna had helped at various household tasks ever since her arrival at the Settlement, for there was no room for drones in the Shaker hive; but after a few weeks in the kitchen with Martha, the herb-garden had been assigned to her as her particular province, the Sisters thinking her better fitted for it than for the preserving and pickling of fruit, or the basket-weaving that needed special apprenticeship.

The Shakers were the first people to raise, put up, and sell garden seeds in our present-day fashion, and it was they, too, who began the preparation of botanical medicines, raising, gathering, drying, and preparing herbs and roots for market; and this industry, driven from the field by modern machinery, was still a valuable source of income in Susanna's day. Plants had always grown for Susanna, and she loved them like friends, humoring their weakness, nourishing their strength, stimulating, coaxing, disciplining them, until they could do no less than flourish under her kind and hopeful hand.

Oh, that sweet, honest, comforting little garden of herbs, with its wholesome fragrances! Healing lay in every root and stem, in every leaf and bud, and the strong aromatic odors stimulated her flagging spirit or her aching head, after the sleepless nights in which she tried to decide her future life and Sue's.

The plants were set out in neat rows and clumps, and she soon learned to know the strange ones—chamomile, lobelia, bloodroot, wormwood, lovage, boneset, lemon and sweet balm, lavender and rue, as well as she knew the old acquaintances familiar to every country-bred child—pennyroyal, peppermint or spearmint, yellow dock, and thoroughwort.

There was hoeing and weeding before the gathering and drying came; then Brother Calvin, who had charge of the great press, would moisten the dried herbs and press them into quarter and half-pound cakes ready for Sister Martha, who would superintend the younger Shakeresses in papering and labeling them for the market. Last of all, when harvesting was over, Brother Ansel would mount the newly painted seed-cart and leave on his driving trip through the country. Ansel was a capital salesman, but Brother Issachar, who once took his place and sold almost nothing, brought home a lad on the seed-cart, who afterward became a shining light in the community. ("Thus," said Elder Gray, "does God teach us the diversity of gifts, whereby all may be unashamed.")

33

If the Albion Shakers were honest and ardent in faith, Susanna thought that their "works" would indeed bear the strictest examination. The Brothers made brooms, floor and dish mops, tubs, pails, and churns, and indeed almost every trade was represented in the various New England Communities. Physicians there were, a few, but no lawyers, sheriffs, policemen, constables, or soldiers, just as there were no courts or saloons or jails. Where there was perfect equality of possession and no private source of gain, it amazed Susanna to see the cheery labor, often continued late at night from the sheer joy of it, and the earnest desire to make the Settlement prosperous. While the Brothers were hammering, nailing, planing, sawing, ploughing, and seeding, the Sisters were carding and spinning cotton, wool, and flax, making kerchiefs of linen, straw Shaker bonnets, and dozens of other useful marketable things, not forgetting their famous Shaker apple sauce.

Was there ever such a busy summer, Susanna wondered; yet with all the early rising, constant labor, and simple fare, she was stronger and hardier than she had been for years. The Shaker palate was never tickled with delicacies, yet the food was well cooked and sufficiently varied. At first there had been the winter vegetables: squash, yellow turnips, beets, and parsnips, with once a week a special Shaker dinner of salt codfish, potatoes, onions, and milk gravy. Each Sister served her turn as cook, but all alike had a wonderful hand with flour, and the whole-wheat bread, cookies, ginger cake, and milk puddings were marvels of lightness. Martha, in particular, could wean the novitiate Shaker from a too riotous devotion to meat-eating better than most people, for every dish she sent to the table was delicate, savory, and attractive.

Dear, patient, devoted Martha! How Susanna learned to love her as they worked together in the big sunny, shining kitchen, where the cooking-stove as well as every tin plate and pan and spoon might have served as a mirror! Martha had joined the Society in her mother's arms, being given up to the Lord and placed in "the children's order" before she was one year old.

"If you should unite with us, Susanna," she said one night after the early supper, when they were peeling apples together, "you'd be thankful you begun early with your little Sue, for she's got a natural attraction to the world, and for it. Not but that she's a tender, loving, obedient little soul; but when she's among the other young ones, there's a flyaway look about her that makes her seem more like a fairy than a child."

"She's having rather a hard time learning Shaker ways, but she'll do better in time," sighed her mother. "She came to me of her own accord yesterday and asked: 'Bettent I have my curls cut off, Mardie?'"

"I never put that idea into her head," Martha interrupted. "She's a visitor and can wear her hair as she's been brought up to wear it."

"I know, but I fear Sue was moved by other than religious reasons. 'I get up so early, Mardie,' she said,—'and it takes so long to unsnarl and untangle me, and I get so hot when I'm helping in the hayfield,—and then I have to be curled for dinner, and curled again for supper, and so it seems like wasting both our times!' Her hair would be all the stronger for cutting, I thought, as it's so long for her age; but I couldn't put the shears to it when the time came, Martha. I had to take her to Eldress Abby. She sat up in front of the little looking-glass as still as a mouse, while the curls came off, but when the last one fell into Abby's apron, she suddenly put her hands over her face and cried: 'Oh, Mardie, we shall never be the same togedder, you and I, after this!'—She seemed to see her 'little past,' her childhood, slipping away from her, all in an instant. I didn't let her know that I cried over the box of curls last night!"

"You did wrong," rebuked Martha. "You shouldn't make an idol of your child or your child's beauty."

"You don't think God might put beauty into the world just to give His children joy, Martha?"

Martha was no controversialist. She had taken her opinions, ready-made, from those she considered her superiors, and although she was willing to make any sacrifice for her religion, she did not wish to be confused by too many opposing theories of God's intentions.

"You know I never argue when I've got anything baking," she said; and taking the spill of a corn-broom from a table-drawer, she opened the oven door and delicately plunged it into the loaf. Then, gazing at the straw as she withdrew it, she said: "You must talk doctrine with Eldress Abby, Susanna, not with me; but I guess doctrine won't help you so much as thinking out your life for yourself."

"No one can sing my psalm for me,Reward must come from labor,I'll sow for peace, and reap in truthGod's mercy and His favor!"
Martha was the chief musician of the Community, and had composed many hymns and tunes—some of them under circumstances that she believed might entitle them to be considered directly inspired. Her clear full voice filled the

kitchen and floated out into the air after Susanna, as she called Sue and, darning-basket in hand, walked across the road to the great barn.

The herb-garden was one place where she could think out her life, although no decision had as yet been born of those thoughtful mornings.

Another spot for meditation was the great barn, relic of the wonderful earlier days, and pride of the present Settlement. A hundred and seventy-five feet long and three and a half stories high, it dominated the landscape. First, there was the cellar, where all the refuse fell, to do its duty later on in fertilizing the farm lands; then came the first floor, where the stalls for horses, oxen, and cows lined the walls on either side. Then came the second floor, where hay was kept, and to reach this a bridge forty feet long was built on stone piers ten feet in height, sloping up from the ground to the second story. Over the easy slope of this bridge the full haycarts were driven, to add their several burdens to the golden haymows. High at the top was an enormous grain room, where mounds of yellow corn-ears reached from floor to ceiling; and at the back was a great window opening on Massabesic Pond and Knights' Hill, with the White Mountains towering blue or snow-capped in the distance. There was an old-fashioned, list-bottomed, straight-backed Shaker chair in front of the open window, a chair as uncomfortable as Shaker doctrines to the daughter of Eve, and there Susanna often sat with her sewing or mending, Sue at her feet building castles out of corn-cobs, plaiting the husks into little mats, or taking out basting threads from her mother's work.

"My head feels awfully undressed without my curls, Mardie," she said. "I'm most afraid Fardie won't like the looks of me; do you think we ought to have asked him before we shingled me?—He does *despise* un-pretty things so!"

"I think if we had asked him he would have said, 'Do as you think best.'"

"He always says that when he doesn't care what you do," observed Sue, with one of her startling bursts of intuition. "Sister Martha has a printed card on the wall in the children's dining-room, and I've got to learn all the poetry on it because I need it worse than any of the others:—

"What we deem good order, we're willing to state,Eat hearty and decent, and clear out your plate;Be thankful to heaven for what we receive,And not make a mixture or compound to leave.
"We often find left on the same China dish,Meat, apple sauce, pickle, brown bread and minced fish:Another's replenished with butter and cheese,With pie, cake, and toast, perhaps, added to these."

"You say it very nicely," commended Susanna.

"There's more:—

"Now if any virtue in this can be shown,By peasant, by lawyer, or king on the throne;We freely will forfeit whatever we've said,And call it a virtue to waste meat and bread."
"There's a great deal to learn when you're being a Shaker," sighed Sue, as she finished her rhyme.

"There's a great deal to learn everywhere," her mother answered. "What verse did Eldress Abby give you to-day?"

"For little tripping maids may follow GodAlong the ways that saintly feet have trod,"
quoted the child. "Am I a tripping maid, Mardie?" she continued.

"Yes, dear."

"If I trip too much, mightn't I fall?"

"Yes, I suppose so."

"Is tripping the same as skipping?"

"About the same."

"Is it polite to tripanskip when you're following God?"

"It couldn't be impolite if you meant to be good. A tripping maid means just a young one."

"What is a maid?"

"A little girl."

"When a maid grows up, what is she?"

"Why—she's a maiden, I suppose."

"When a maiden grows up, what is *she*?"

"Just a woman, Sue."

"What is saintly feet?"

"Feet like those of Eldress Abby or Elder Gray; feet of people who have always tried to do right."

"Are Brother Ansel's feet saintly?"

"He's a good, kind, hard-working man."

"Is good-kind-hard-working same as saintly?"

"Well, it's not so very different, perhaps.—Now, Sue, I've asked you before, don't let your mind grope, and your little tongue wag, every instant; it isn't good for you, and it certainly isn't good for me!"

"All right; but 'less I gropeanwag sometimes, I don't see how I'll ever learn the things I 'specially want to know?" sighed Sue the insatiable.

"Shall I tell you a Shaker story, one that Eldress Abby told me last evening?"

"Oh, do, Mardie!" cried Sue, crossing her feet, folding her hands, and looking up into her mother's face expectantly.

"Once there was a very good Shaker named Elder Calvin Green, and some one wrote him a letter asking him to come a long distance and found a Settlement in the western part of New York State. He and some other Elders and Eldresses traveled five days, and stopped at the house of a certain Joseph Pelham to spend Sunday and hold a meeting. On Monday morning, very tired, and wondering where to stay and begin his preaching, the Elder went out into the woods to pray for guidance. When he rose from his knees, feeling stronger and lighter-hearted, a young quail came up to him so close that he picked it up. It was not a bit afraid, neither did the old parent birds who were standing near by show any sign of fear, though they are very timid creatures. The Elder smoothed the young bird's feathers a little while and then let it go, but he thought an angel seemed to say to him, 'The quail is a sign; you will know before night what it means, and before to-morrow people will be coming to you to learn the way to God.'

"Soon after, a flock of these shy little birds alighted on Joseph Pelham's house, and the Elders were glad, and thought it signified the flock of Believers that would gather in that place; for the Shakers see more in signs than other people. Just at night a young girl of twelve or thirteen knocked at the door and told Elder Calvin that she wanted to become a Shaker, and that her father and mother were willing.

"'Here is the little quail!' cried the Elder, and indeed she was the first who flocked to the meetings and joined the new Community.

"On their return to their old home across the state the Elders took the little quail girl with them. It was November then, and the canals through which they traveled were clogged with ice. One night, having been ferried across the Mohawk River, they took their baggage and walked for miles before they could find shelter. Finally, when they were within three miles of their home, Elder Calvin shortened the way by going across the open fields through the snow, up and down the hills and through the gullies and over fences, till they reached the house at midnight, safe and sound, the brave little quail girl having trudged beside them the whole distance, carrying her tin pail."

Sue was transported with interest, her lips parted, her eyes shining, her hands clasped.

"Oh, I wish I could be a brave little quail girl, Mardie! What became of her?"

"Her name was Polly Reed, and when she grew up, she became a teacher of the Shaker school, then an Eldress, and even a preacher. I don't know what kind of a little quail girl you would make, Sue; do you think you could walk for miles through the ice and snow uncomplainingly?"

"I don' know's I could," sighed Sue; "but," she added hopefully, "perhaps I could teach or preach, and then I could gropeanwag as much as ever I liked." Then, after a lengthy pause, in which her mind worked feverishly, she said, "Mardie, I was just groping a little bit, but I won't do it any more to-night. If the old quail birds in the woods where Elder Calvin prayed, if those old birds had been Shaker birds, there wouldn't have been any little quail birds, would there, because Shakers don't have children, and then perhaps there wouldn't have been any little Polly Reed."

Susanna rose hurriedly from the list-bottomed chair and folded her work. "I'll go up and help you undress now," she said; "it's seven o'clock, and I must go to the family meeting."

VI

IT was the Sabbath day and the Believers were gathered in the meeting-house, Brethren and Sisters seated quietly on their separate benches, with the children by themselves in their own place. As the men entered the room they removed their hats and coats and hung them upon wooden pegs that lined the sides of the room, while the women took off their bonnets; then, after standing for a moment of perfect silence, they seated themselves.

In Susanna's time the Sunday costume for the men included trousers of deep blue cloth with a white line and a vest of darker blue, exposing a full-bosomed shirt that had a wide turned-down collar fastened with three buttons. The Sisters were in pure white dresses, with neck and shoulders covered with snowy kerchiefs, their heads crowned with their white net caps, and a large white pocket handkerchief hung over the left arm. Their feet were shod with curious pointed-toed cloth shoes of ultramarine blue—a fashion long since gone by.

Susanna had now become accustomed to the curious solemn march or dance in which of course none but the Believers ever joined, and found in her present exalted mood the songs and the exhortations strangely interesting and not unprofitable.

Tabitha, the most aged of the group of Albion Sisters, confessed that she missed the old times when visions were common, when the Spirit manifested itself in extraordinary ways, and the gift of tongues descended. Sometimes, in the Western Settlement where she was gathered in, the whole North Family would march into the highway in the fresh morning hours, and while singing some sacred hymn, would pass on to the Centre Family, and together in solemn yet glad procession they would mount the hillside to "Jehovah's Chosen Square," there to sing and dance before the Lord.

"I wish we could do something like that now!" sighed Hetty Arnold, a pretty young creature, who had moments of longing for the pomps and vanities. "If we have to give up all worldly pleasures, I think we might have more religious ones!"

"We were a younger church in those old times of which Sister Tabitha speaks," said Eldress Abby. "You must remember, Hetty, that we were children in faith, and needed signs and manifestations, pictures and object-lessons. We've been trained to think and reason now, and we've put away some of our picture-books. There have been revelations to tell us we needed movements and exercises to quicken our spiritual powers, and to give energy and unity to our worship, and there have been revelations telling us to give them up; revelations bidding us to sing more, revelations telling us to use wordless songs. Then anthems were given us, and so it has gone on, for we have been led of the Spirit."

"I'd like more picture-books," pouted Hetty, under her breath.

To-day the service began with a solemn song, followed by speaking and prayer from a visiting elder. Then, after a long and profound silence, the company rose and joined in a rhythmic dance which signified the onward travel of the soul to full redemption; the opening and closing of the hands meaning the scattering and gathering of blessing. There was no accompaniment, and both the music and the words were the artless expression of fervent devotion.

SUSANNA SAT IN HER CORNER BESIDE
THE AGED TABITHA

Susanna sat in her corner beside the aged Tabitha, who would never dance again before the Lord, though her quavering voice joined in the chorus. The spring floor rose and fell under the quick rhythmic tread of the worshipers, and with each revolution about the room the song gained in power and fervor.

The steps grew slower and more sedate, the voices died away, the arms sank slowly by the sides, and the hands ceased their movement.

Susanna rose to her feet, she knew not how or why. Her cheeks were flushed, her head bent.

"Dear friends," she said, "I have now been among you for nearly three months, sharing your life, your work, and your worship. You may well wish to know whether I have made up my mind to join this Community, and I can only say that although I have prayed for light, I cannot yet see my way clearly. I am happy here with you, and although I have been a church member for years, I have never before longed so ardently to present my body and soul as a sacrifice unto the Lord. I have tried not to be a burden to you. The small weekly sum that I put into the treasury I will not speak of, lest I seem to think that the 'gift of God may be purchased with money,' as the Scriptures say; but I have endeavored to be loyal to your rules and customs, your aims and ideals, and to the confidence you have reposed in me. Oh, my dear Sisters and Brothers, pray for me that I be enabled to see my duty more plainly. It is not the flesh-pots that will call me back to the world; if I go, it will be because the duties I have left behind take such shape that they draw me out of this shelter in spite of myself. I thank you for the help you have given me these last weeks; God knows my gratitude can never be spoken in words."

Elder Gray's voice broke the silence that followed Susanna's speech. "I only echo the sentiments of the Family when I say that our Sister Susanna shall have such time as she requires before deciding to unite with this body of Believers. No pressure shall be brought to bear upon her, and she will be, as she ever has been, a welcome guest under our roof. She has been an inspiration to the children, a comfort and aid to the Sisters, an intelligent comrade to the Brethren, and a sincere and earnest student of the truth. May the Spirit draw her into the Virgin Church of the New Creation!"

"Yee and amen!" exclaimed Eldress Abby, devoutly: "For thus saith the Lord of hosts: I will shake the heavens, and the earth, and the sea, and the dry land; and I will shake all nations, and the desire of all nations shall come: and I will fill this house with glory, saith the Lord of hosts."

"O Virgin Church, how great thy light,What cloud can dim thy way?"
sang Martha from her place at the end of a bench; and all the voices took up the hymn softly as the company sat with bowed heads.

Then Brother Issachar rose from his corner, saying: "Jesus called upon his disciples to give up everything: houses, lands, relationships, and even the selfishness of their own lives. They could not call their lives their own. '*Lo! we have left all and followed thee,*' said Peter; 'fathers, mothers, wives, children, houses, lands, and even our own lives also.' It is a great price to pay, but we buy Heaven with it!"

"Yee, we do," said Brother Thomas Scattergood, devoutly. "To him that overcometh shall the great prize be given."

"God help the weaker brethren!" murmured young Brother Nathan, in so low a voice that few could hear him.

Moved by the same impulse, Tabitha, Abby, and Martha burst into one of the most triumphant of the Shaker songs, one that was never sung save when the meeting was "full of the Spirit":—

"I draw no blank nor miss the prize,I see the work, the sacrifice,And I'll be loyal, I'll be wise,A faithful overcomer!"
The company rose and began again to march in a circle around the centre of the room, the Brethren two abreast leading the column, the Sisters following after. There was a waving movement of the hands by drawing inward as if gathering in spiritual good and storing it up for future need. In the marching and countermarching the worshipers frequently changed their positions, ultimately forming into four circles, symbolical of the four dispensations as expounded in Shakerism, the first from Adam to Abraham; the second from Abraham to Jesus; the third from Jesus to Mother Ann Lee; and the fourth the millennial era.

The marching grew livelier; the bodies of the singers swayed lightly with emotion, the faces glowed with feeling.

Over and over the hymn was sung, gathering strength and fullness as the Believers entered more and more into the spirit of their worship. Whenever the refrain came in with its militant fervor, crude, but sincere and effective, the singers seemed faith-intoxicated; and Sister Martha in particular might have been treading the heavenly streets instead of the meeting-house floor, so complete was her absorption. The voices at length grew softer, and the movement slower, and after a few moments' reverent silence the company filed out of the room solemnly and without speech.

"The Lord ain't shaken Susanna hard enough yet," thought Brother Ansel shrewdly from his place in the rear. "She ain't altogether gathered in, not by no manner o' means, because of that unregenerate son of Adam she's left behind; but there's the makin's of a pow'ful good Shaker in Susanna, if she finally takes holt!"

"What manner of life is my husband living, now that I have deserted him? Who is being a mother to Jack?" These were the thoughts that troubled Susanna Hathaway's soul as she crossed the grass to her own building.

VII

BROTHER Nathan Bennett was twenty years old and Sister Hetty Arnold was eighteen. They had been left with the Shakers by their respective parents ten years before, and, growing up in the faith, they formally joined the Community when they reached the age of discretion. Thus they had known each other from early childhood, never in the familiar way common to the children of the world, but with the cool, cheerful, casual, wholly impersonal attitude of Shaker friendship, a relation seemingly outside of and superior to sex, a relation more like that of two astral bodies than the more intimate one of a budding Adam and Eve.

When and where had this relationship changed its color and meaning? Neither Nathan nor Hetty could have told. For years Nathan had sat at his end of the young men's bench at the family or the public meeting, with Hetty exactly opposite him at the end of the girls' row, and for years they had looked across the dividing space at each other with unstirred pulses. The rows of Sisters sat in serene dignity, one bench behind another, and each Sister was like unto every other in Nathan's vague, dreamy, boyishly indifferent eyes. Some of them were seventy and some seventeen, but each modest figure sat in its place with quiet folded hands. The stiff caps hid the hair, whether it was silver or gold; the white surplices covered the shoulders and concealed beautiful curves as well as angular outlines; the throats were scarcely visible, whether they were yellow and wrinkled or young and white. The Sisters were simply sisters to fair-haired Nathan, and the Brothers were but brothers to little black-eyed Hetty.

Once—was it on a Sunday morning?—Nathan glanced across the separating space that is the very essence and sign of Shakerism. The dance had just ceased, and there was a long, solemn stillness when God indeed seemed to be in one of His holy temples and the earth was keeping silence before Him. Suddenly Hetty grew to be something more than one of the figures in a long row: she chained Nathan's eye and held it.

"Through her garments the grace of her glowed." He saw that, in spite of the way her hair had been cut and stretched back from the forehead, a short dusky tendril, softened and coaxed by the summer heat, had made its way mutinously beyond the confines of her cap. Her eyes were cast down, but the lashes that swept her round young cheek were quite different from any other lashes in the Sisters' row. Her breath came and went softly after the exertion of the rhythmic movements, stirring the white muslin folds that wrapped her from throat to waist. He looked and looked, until his body seemed to be all eyes, absolutely unaware of any change in himself; quite oblivious of the fact that he was regarding the girl in any new and dangerous way.

The silence continued, long and profound, until suddenly Hetty raised her beautiful lashes and met Nathan's gaze, the gaze of a boy just turned to man: ardent, warm, compelling. There was a startled moment of recognition, a tremulous approach, almost an embrace, of regard; each sent an electric current across the protective separating space, the two pairs of eyes met and said, "I love you," in such clear tones that Nathan and Hetty marveled that the Elder did not hear them. Somebody says that love, like a scarlet spider, can spin a thread between two hearts almost in an instant, so fine as to be almost invisible, yet it will hold with the tenacity of an iron chain. The thread had been spun; it was so delicate that neither Nathan nor Hetty had seen the scarlet spider spinning it, but the strength of both would not avail to snap the bond that held them together.

The moments passed. Hetty's kerchief rose and fell, rose and fell tumultuously, while her face was suffused with color. Nathan's knees quivered under him, and when the Elder rose, and they began the sacred march, the lad could hardly stand for trembling. He dreaded the moment when the lines of Believers would meet, and he and Hetty would walk the length of the long room almost beside each other. Could she hear his heart beating, Nathan wondered; while Hetty was palpitating with fear lest Nathan see her blushes and divine their meaning. Oh, the joy of it, the terror of it, the strange exhilaration and the sudden sensation of sin and remorse!

The meeting over, Nathan flung himself on the haymow in the great barn, while Hetty sat with her "Synopsis of Shaker Theology" at an open window of the girls' building, seeing nothing in the lines of print but visions that should not have been there. It was Nathan who felt most and suffered most and was most conscious of sin, for Hetty, at first, scarcely knew whither she was drifting.

She went into the herb-garden with Susanna one morning during the week that followed the fatal Sunday. Many of the plants to be used for seasoning— sage, summer savory, sweet marjoram, and the like—were quite ready for gathering. As the two women were busy at work, Susanna as full of her thoughts as Hetty of hers, the sound of a step was heard brushing the grass of the orchard. Hetty gave a nervous start; her cheeks grew so crimson and her breath so short that Susanna noticed the change.

"It will be Brother Ansel coming along to the grindstone," Hetty stammered, burying her head in the leaves.

"No," Susanna answered, "it is Nathan. He has a long pole with a saw on the end. He must be going to take the dead branches off the apple trees; I heard Ansel tell him yesterday to do it."

"Yee, that will be it," said Hetty, bending over the plants as if she were afraid to look elsewhere.

Nathan came nearer to the herb-garden. He was a tall, stalwart, handsome enough fellow, even in his quaint working garb. As the Sisters spun and wove the cloth as well as cut and made the men's garments, and as the Brothers themselves made the shoes, there was naturally no great air of fashion about the Shaker raiment; but Nathan carried it better than most. His skin was fair and rosy, the down on his upper lip showed dawning manhood, and when he took off his broad-brimmed straw hat and stretched to his full height to reach the upper branches of the apple trees, he made a picture of clean, wholesome, vigorous youth.

Suddenly Susanna raised her head and surprised Hetty looking at the lad with all her heart in her eyes. At the same moment Nathan turned, and before he could conceal the telltale ardor of his glance, it had sped to Hetty. With the instinct of self-preservation he stooped instantly as if to steady the saw on the pole, but it was too late to mend matters: his tale was told so far as Susanna was concerned; but it was better she should suspect than one of the Believers or Eldress Abby.

HETTY LOOKING AT THE LAD WITH ALL
HER HEART IN HER EYES

Susanna worked on in silent anxiety. The likelihood of such crises as this had sometimes crossed her mind, and knowing how frail human nature is, she often marveled that instances seemed so infrequent. Her instinct told her that in every Community the risk must exist, even though all were doubly warned and armed against the temptations that flesh is heir to; yet no hint of danger had showed itself during the months in which she had been a member of the Shaker family. She had heard the Elder's plea to the young converts to take up "a full cross against the flesh"; she had listened to Eldress Abby when she told them that the natural life, its thoughts, passions, feelings, and associations, must be turned against once and forever; but her heart melted in pity for the two poor young things struggling helplessly against instincts of which they hardly knew the meaning, so cloistered had been the life they lived.

The kind, conscientious hands that had fed them would now seem hard and unrelenting; the place that had been home would turn to a prison; the life that Elder Gray preached, "the life of a purer godliness than can be attained by marriage," had seemed difficult, perhaps, but possible; and now how cold and hopeless it would appear to these two young, undisciplined, flaming hearts!

"Hetty dear, talk to me!" whispered Susanna, softly touching her shoulder, and wondering if she could somehow find a way to counsel the girl in her perplexity.

Hetty started rebelliously to her feet as Nathan moved away farther into the orchard. "If you say a single thing to me, or a word about me to Eldress Abby, I'll run away this very day. Nobody has any right to speak to me, and I just want to be let alone! It's all very well for you," she went on passionately. "What have you had to give up? Nothing but a husband you didn't love and a home you didn't want to stay in. Like as not you'll be a Shaker, and they'll take you for a saint; but anyway you'll have had your life."

"You are right, Hetty," said Susanna, quietly; "but oh! my dear, the world outside isn't such a Paradise for young girls like you, motherless and fatherless and penniless. You have a good home here; can't you learn to like it?"

"Out in the world people can do as they like and nobody thinks of calling them wicked!" sobbed Hetty, flinging herself down, and putting her head in Susanna's aproned lap. "Here you've got to live like an angel, and if you don't, you've got to confess every wrong thought you've had, when the time comes."

"Whatever you do, Hetty, be open and aboveboard; don't be hasty and foolish, or you may be sorry forever afterwards."

Hetty's mood changed again suddenly to one of mutiny, and she rose to her feet.

"You haven't got any right to interfere with me anyway, Susanna; and if you think it's your duty to tell tales, you'll only make matters worse"; and so saying she took her basket and fled across the fields like a hunted hare.

That evening, as Hetty left the infirmary, where she had been sent with a bottle of liniment for the nursing Sisters, she came upon Nathan standing gloomily under the spruce trees near the back of the building. It was eight o'clock and quite dark. It had been raining during the late afternoon and the trees were still dripping drearily. Hetty came upon Nathan so suddenly, that, although he had been in her thoughts, she gave a frightened little cry when he drew her peremptorily under the shadow of the branches. The rules that govern the Shaker Community are very strict, but in reality the true Believer never thinks of them as rules, nor is trammeled by them. They are fixed habits of the blood, as common, as natural, as sitting or standing, eating or drinking. No Brother is allowed to hold any lengthy interview with a Sister, nor to work, walk, or drive with her alone; but these protective customs, which all are bound in honor to keep, are too much a matter of every-day life to be strange or irksome.

"I must speak to you, Hetty," whispered Nathan. "I cannot bear it any longer alone. What shall we do?"

"Do?" echoed Hetty, trembling.

"Yes, *do*." There was no pretense of asking her if she loved or suffered, or lived in torture and suspense. They had not uttered a word to each other, but their eyes had "shed meanings."

"You know we can't go on like this," he continued rapidly. "We can't eat their food, stay alongside of them, pray their prayers and act a lie all the time,— we *can't!*"

"Nay, we can't!" said Hetty. "Oh, Nathan, shall we confess all and see if they will help us to resist temptation? I know that's what Susanna would want me to do, but oh! I should dread it."

"Nay, it is too late," Nathan answered drearily. "They could not help us, and we should be held under suspicion forever after."

"I feel so wicked and miserable and unfaithful, I don't know what to do!" sobbed Hetty.

"Yee, so do I!" the lad answered. "And I feel bitter against my father, too. He brought me here to get rid of me, because he didn't dare leave me on somebody's doorstep. He ought to have come back when I was grown a man and asked me if I felt inclined to be a Shaker, and if I was good enough to be one!"

"And my stepfather wouldn't have me in the house, so my mother had to give me away; but they're both dead, and I'm alone in the world, though I've never felt it, because the Sisters are so kind. Now they will hate me—though they don't hate anybody."

"You've got me, Hetty! We must go away and be married. We'd better go to-night to the minister in Albion."

"What if he wouldn't do it?"

"Why shouldn't he? Shakers take no vows, though I feel bound, hand and foot, out of gratitude. If any other two young folks went to him, he would marry them; and if he refuses, there are two other ministers in Albion, besides two more in Buryfield, five miles farther. If they won't marry us to-night, I'll leave you in some safe home and we'll walk to Portland to-morrow. I'm young and strong, and I know I can earn our living somehow."

"But we haven't the price of a lodging or a breakfast between us," Hetty said tearfully. "Would it be sinful to take some of my basket-work and send back the money next week?"

"Yee, it would be so," Nathan answered sternly. "The least we can do is to go away as empty-handed as we came. I can work for our breakfast."

"Oh, I can't bear to disappoint Eldress Abby," cried Hetty, breaking anew into tears. "She'll say we've run away to live on the lower plane after agreeing to crucify Nature and follow the angelic life!"

"I know; but there are five hundred people in Albion all living in marriage, and we shan't be the only sinners!" Nathan argued. "Oh, Sister Hetty, dear Hetty, keep up your spirits and trust to me!"

Nathan's hand stole out and met Hetty's in its warm clasp, the first hand touch that the two ignorant young creatures had ever felt. Nathan's knowledge of life had been a journey to the Canterbury Shakers in New Hampshire with Brother Issachar; Hetty's was limited to a few drives into Albion village, and half a dozen chats with the world's people who came to the Settlement to buy basket-work.

"I am not able to bear the Shaker life!" sighed Nathan. "Elder Gray allows there be such!"

"Nor I," murmured Hetty. "Eldress Harriet knows I am no saint!"

Hetty's head was now on Nathan's shoulder. The stiff Shaker cap had resisted bravely, but the girl's head had yielded to the sweet proximity. Youth called to youth triumphantly; the Spirit was unheard, and all the theories of celibacy and the angelic life that had been poured into their ears vanished into thin air. The thick shade of the spruce tree hid the kiss that would have been so innocent, had they not given themselves to the Virgin Church; the drip, drip, drip of the branches on their young heads passed unheeded.

Then, one following the other silently along the highroad, hurrying along in the shadows of the tall trees, stealing into the edge of the woods, or hiding behind a thicket of alders at the fancied sound of a footstep or the distant rumble of a wagon, Nathan and Hetty forsook the faith of Mother Ann and went out into the world as Adam and Eve left the garden, with the knowledge of good and evil implanted in their hearts. The voice of Eldress Abby pursued Hetty in her flight like the voice in a dream. She could hear its clear impassioned accents, saying, "The children of this world marry; but the children of the resurrection do not marry, for they are as the angels." The solemn tones grew fainter and fainter as Hetty's steps led her farther and farther away from the quiet Shaker village and its drab-clad Sisters, and at last they almost died into silence, because Nathan's voice was nearer and Nathan's voice was dearer.

VIII

THERE was no work in the herb-garden now, but there was never a moment from dawn till long after dusk when the busy fingers of the Shaker Sisters were still. When all else failed there was the knitting: socks for the Brothers and stockings for the Sisters and socks and stockings of every size for the children. One of the quaint sights of the Settlement to Susanna was the clump of young Sisters on the porch of the girls' building, knitting, knitting, in the afternoon sun. Even little Shaker Jane and Mary, Maria and Lucinda, had their socks in hand, and plied their short knitting-needles soberly and not unskillfully. The sight of their industry incited the impetuous Sue to effort, and under the patient tutelage of Sister Martha she mastered the gentle art. Susanna never forgot the hour when, coming from her work in the seed-room, she crossed the grass with a message to Martha, and saw the group of children and girls on the western porch, a place that caught every ray of afternoon sun, the last glint of twilight, and the first hint of sunset glow. Sister Martha had been reading the Sabbath-school lesson for the next day, and as Susanna neared the building, Martha's voice broke into a hymn. Falteringly the girls' voices followed the lead, uncertain at first of words or tune, but gaining courage and strength as they went on:—

"As the waves of the mighty oceanGospel love we will circulate,And as we give, in due proportion,We of the heavenly life partake.Heavenly Life, Glorious Life,Resurrecting, Soul-Inspiring,Re-gen-er-a-ting Gospel Life,Itleadeth away from all sin and strife!"

The clear, innocent treble sounded sweetly in the virgin stillness and solitude of the Settlement, and as Susanna drew closer she stopped under a tree to catch the picture—Sister Martha, grave, tall, discreet, singing with all her soul and marking time with her hands, so accustomed to the upward and downward movement of the daily service. The straight, plain dresses were as fresh and smooth as perfect washing could make them, and the round childlike faces looked quaint and sweet with the cropped hair tucked under the stiff little caps. Sue was seated with Mary and Jane on the steps, and Susanna saw with astonishment that her needles were moving to and fro and she was knitting as serenely and correctly as a mother in Israel; singing, too, in a delicate little treble that was like a skylark's morning note. Susanna could hear her distinctly as she delightedly flung out the long words so dear to her soul and so difficult to dull little Jane and Mary:—

"Res-ur-rect-ing, Soul-In-spir-ing,Re-gen-er-a-ting Gospel Life,It lead-eth a-way from all sin and strife."

Jane's cap was slightly unsettled, causing its wearer to stop knitting now and then and pull it forward or push it back; and in one of these little feminine difficulties Susanna saw Sue reach forward and deftly transfer the cap to her own head. Jane was horrified, but rather slow to wrath and equally slow in ingenuity. Sue looked a delicious Shaker with her delicate face, her lovely eyes, and her yellow hair grown into soft rings; and quite intoxicated with her cap, her knitting, and the general air of holiness so unexpectedly emanating from her, she moved her little hands up and down, as the tune rose and fell, in a way that would have filled Eldress Abby with joy. Susanna's heart beat fast, and she wondered for a moment, as she went back to her room, whether she could ever give Sue a worldly childhood more free from danger than the life she was now living. She found letters from Aunt Louisa and Jack on reaching her room, and they lay in her lap under a pile of towels, to be read and reread while her busy needle flew over the coarse crash. Sue stole in quietly, kissed her mother's cheek, and sat down on her stool by the window, marveling, with every "under" of the needle and "over" of the yarn, that it was she, Sue Hathaway, who was making a real stocking.

Jack's pen was not that of an especially ready writer, but he had a practical way of conveying considerable news. His present contributions, when freed from their phonetic errors and spelled in Christian fashion, read somewhat as follows:—

Father says I must write to you every week, even if I make him do without, so I will. I am well, and so is Aunt Louisa, and any boy that lives with her has to toe the mark, I tell you; but she is good and has fine things to eat every meal. What did Sue get for her birthday? I got a book from father and one from Aunt Louisa and the one from you that you told her to buy. It is queer that people will give a boy books when he has only one knife, and that a broken one. There's a book prize to be given at the school, and I am pretty afraid I will get that, too; it would be just my luck. Teachers think about nothing but books and what good they do, but I heard of a boy that had a grand knife with five sharp blades and a corkscrew, and in a shipwreck he cut all the ropes, so the sail came down that was carrying them on to the rocks, and then by boring a hole with his corkscrew all the water leaked out of the ship that had been threatening to sink the sailors. I could use a little pocket money, as Aunt Louisa keeps me short.... I have been spending Sunday with father, and had a pretty good time, not so very. Father will take me about more when he stops going to the store, which will be next week for good. The kitchen floor is new painted, and Ellen says it sticks, and Aunt Louisa is going to make Ellen clean house in case you come home. Do you like where you are? Our teacher told the girls' teacher it seemed a long stay for any one who had a family, and the boys at school call me a half orphan and say my mother has left me and so my father has to board me in the country. My money is run out again. I sat down in a puddle this afternoon, but it dried up pretty quick and didn't hurt my clothes, so no more from your son

JACK.

This was the sort of message that had been coming to Susanna of late, bringing up little pictures of home duties and responsibilities, homely tasks and trials. "John giving up the store for good"; what did that mean? Had he gone from bad to worse in the solitude that she had hoped might show him the gravity of his offenses, the error of his ways? In case she should die, what then would become of the children? Would Louisa accept the burden of Jack, for whom she had never cared? Would the Shakers take Sue? She would be safe; perhaps she would always be happy; but brother and sister would be divided and brought up as strangers. Would little Sue, grown to big Sue, say some time or other, "My mother renounced the world for herself, but what right had she to renounce it for me? Why did she rob me of the dreams of girlhood and the natural hopes of women, when I was too young to give consent?" These and other unanswerable questions continually drifted through Susanna's mind, disturbing its balance and leaving her like a shuttlecock bandied to and fro between conflicting blows.

"Mardie," came a soft little voice from across the room; "Mardie, what is a backslider?"

"Where did you hear that long word, Sue?" asked Susanna, rousing herself from her dream.

"'Tisn't so long as 'regenerating' and more easier."

"Regenerating means 'making over,' you know."

"There'd ought to be children's words and grown-up words,—that's what *I* think," said Sue, decisively; "but what does 'backslider' mean?"

"A backslider is one who has been climbing up a hill and suddenly begins to slip back."

"Doesn't his feet take hold right, or why does he slip?"

"Perhaps he can't manage his feet; perhaps they just won't climb."

53

"Yes, or p'raps he just doesn't want to climb any more; but it must be frightensome, sliding backwards."

"I suppose it is."

"Is it wicked?"

"Why, yes, it is, generally; perhaps always."

"Brother Nathan and Sister Hetty were backsliders; Sister Tabitha said so. She told Jane never to speak their names again any more than if they was dead."

"Then you had better not speak of them, either."

"There's so many things better not to speak of in the world, sometimes I think 'twould be nicer to be an angel."

"Nicer, perhaps, but one has to be very good to be an angel."

"Backsliders couldn't be angels, I s'pose?"

"Not while they were backsliders; but perhaps they'd begin to climb again, and then in time they might grow to be angels."

"I shouldn't think likely," remarked Sue, decisively, clicking her needles as one who could settle most spiritual problems in a jiffy. "I think the sliding kind is diff'rent from the climbing kind, and they don't make easy angels."

A long pause followed this expression of opinion, this simple division of the human race, at the start, into sheep and goats. Then presently the untiring voice broke the stillness again.

"Nathan and Hetty slid back when they went away from here. Did we backslide when we left Fardie and Jack?"

"I'm not sure but that we did," said poor Susanna.

"There's children-Shakers, and brother-and-sister Shakers, but no father-and-mother Shakers?"

"No; they think they can do just as much good in the world without being mothers and fathers."

"Do you think so?"

"Ye-es, I believe I do."

"Well, are you a truly Shaker, or can't you be till you wear a cap?"

"I'm not a Shaker yet, Sue."

"You're just only a mother?"

"Yes, that's about all."

"Maybe we'd better go back to where there's not so many Sisters and more mothers, so you'll have somebody to climb togedder with?"

"I could climb here, Sue, and so could you."

"Yes, but who'll Fardie and Jack climb with? I wish they'd come and see us. Brother Ansel would make Fardie laugh, and Jack would love farm-work, and we'd all be so happy. I miss Fardie awfully! He didn't speak to me much, but I liked to look at his curly hair and think how lovely it would be if he did take notice of me and play with me."

A sob from Susanna brought Sue, startled, to her side.

"You break my heart, Sue! You break it every day with the things you say. Don't you love me, Sue?"

"More'n tongue can tell!" cried Sue, throwing herself into her mother's arms. "Don't cry, darling Mardie! I won't talk any more, not for days and days! Let me wipe your poor eyes. Don't let Elder Gray see you crying, or he'll think I've been naughty. He's just going in downstairs to see Eldress Abby. Was it wrong what I said about backsliding, or what, Mardie? We'll help each udder climb, an' then we'll go home an' help poor lonesome Fardie; shall we?"

"Abby!" called Elder Gray, stepping into the entry of the Office Building.

"Yee, I'm coming," Eldress Abby answered from the stairway. "Go right out and sit down on the bench by the door, where I can catch a few minutes more light for my darning; the days seem to be growing short all to once. Did Lemuel have a good sale of basket-work at the mountains? Rosetta hasn't done so well for years at Old Orchard. We seem to be prospering in every material direction, Daniel, but my heart is heavy somehow, and I have to be instant in prayer to keep from discouragement."

"It hasn't been an altogether good year with us spiritually," confessed Daniel; "perhaps we needed chastening."

"If we needed it, we've received it," Abby ejaculated, as she pushed her darning-ball into the foot of a stocking. "Nothing has happened since I came here thirty years ago that has troubled me like the running away of Nathan and Hetty. If they had been new converts, we should have thought the good seed hadn't got fairly rooted, but those children were brought to us when Nathan was eleven and Hetty nine."

"I well remember, for the boy's father and the girl's mother came on the same train; a most unusual occurrence to receive two children in one day."

"I have cause to remember Hetty in her first month, for she was as wild as a young hawk. She laughed in meeting the first Sunday, and when she came back, I told her to sit behind me in silence for half an hour while I was reading my Bible. 'Be still now, Hetty, and labor to repent,' I said. When the time was up, she said in a meek little mite of a voice, 'I think I'm least in the Kingdom now. Eldress Abby!' 'Then run outdoors,' I said. She kicked up her heels like a colt and was through the door in a second. Not long afterwards I put my hands behind me to tie my apron tighter, and if that child hadn't taken my small scissors lying on the table and cut buttonholes all up and down my strings, hundreds of them, while she was 'laboring to repent.'"

Elder Gray smiled reminiscently, though he had often heard the story before. "Neither of the children came from godly families," he said, "but at least the parents never interfered with us nor came here putting false ideas into their children's heads."

"That's what I say," continued Abby; "and now, after ten years' training and discipline in the angelic life, Hetty being especially promising, to think of their going away together, and worse yet, being married in Albion village right at our very doors; I don't hardly dare to go to bed nights for fear of hearing in the morning that some of the other young folks have been led astray by this foolish performance of Hetty's; I know it was Hetty's fault; Nathan never had ingenuity enough to think and plan it all out."

"Nay, nay, Abby, don't be too hard on the girl; I've watched Nathan closely, and he has been in a dangerous and unstable state, even as long ago as his last confession; but this piece of backsliding, grievous as it is, doesn't cause me as much sorrow as the fall of Brother Ephraim. To all appearance he had conquered his appetite, and for five years he has led a sober life. I had even great hopes of him for the ministry, and suddenly, like a great cloud in the blue sky, has come this terrible visitation, this reappearance of the old Adam. 'Ephraim has returned to his idols.'"

"How have you decided to deal with him, Daniel?"

"It is his first offense since he cast in his lot with us; we must rebuke, chastise, and forgive."

"Yee, yee, I agree to that; but how if he makes us the laughing-stock of the community and drags our sacred banner in the dust? We can't afford to have one of our order picked up in the streets by the world's people."

"Have the world's people found an infallible way to keep those of *their* order out of the gutters?" asked Elder Gray. "Ephraim seems repentant; if he is willing to try again, we must be willing to do as much."

"Yee, Daniel, you are right. Another matter that causes me anxiety is Susanna. I never yearned for a soul as I yearn for hers! She has had the advantage of more education and more reading than most of us have ever enjoyed; she's gifted in teaching and she wins the children. She's discreet and spiritually minded; her life in the world, even with the influence of her dissipated husband, hasn't really stained, only humbled her; she would make such a Shaker, if she was once 'convinced,' as we haven't gathered in for years and years; but I fear she's slipping, slipping away, Daniel!"

"What makes you feel so now, particularly?"

"She's diff'rent as time goes on. She's had more letters from that place where her boy is; she cries nights, and though she doesn't relax a mite with her work, she drags about sometimes like a bird with one wing."

Elder Daniel took off his broad-brimmed hat to cool his forehead and hair, lifting his eyes to the first pale stars that were trembling in the sky, hesitating in silver and then quietly deepening into gold.

Brother Ansel was a Believer because he had no particular love for the world and no great susceptibility to its temptations; but what had drawn Daniel Gray from the open sea into this quiet little backwater of a Shaker Settlement?

After an adventurous early life, in which, as if youth-intoxicated, he had plunged from danger to danger, experience to experience, he suddenly found himself in a society of which he had never so much as heard, a company of celibate brothers and sisters holding all goods and possessions in common, and trying to live the "angelic life" on earth. Illness detained him for a month against his will, but at the end of that time he had joined the Community; and although it had been twenty-five years since his gathering in, he was still steadfast in the faith.

His character was of puritanical sternness; he was a strict disciplinarian, and insisted upon obedience to the rules of Shaker life, "the sacred laws of Zion," as he was wont to term them. He magnified his office, yet he was of a kindly disposition easily approached by children, and not without a quaint old-time humor.

There was a long pause while the two faithful leaders of the little flock were absorbed in thought; then the Elder said: "Susanna's all you say, and the child,—well, if she could be purged of her dross, I never saw a creature better fitted to live the celestial life; but we must not harbor any divided hearts here. When the time comes, we must dismiss her with our blessing."

"Yee, I suppose so," said Eldress Abby, loyally, but it was with a sigh. Had she and Tabitha been left to their own instincts, they would have gone out into the highways and hedges, proselyting with the fervor of Mother Ann's day and generation.

"After all, Abby," said the Elder, rising to take his leave, still in a sort of mild trance,—"after all, Abby, I suppose the Shakers don't own the whole of heaven. I'd like to think so, but I can't. It's a big place, and it belongs to God."

IX

THE woods on the shores of Massabesic Pond were stretches of tapestry, where every shade of green and gold, olive and brown, orange and scarlet, melted the one into the other. The sombre pines made a deep-toned background; patches of sumach gave their flaming crimson; the goldenrod grew rank and tall in glorious profusion, and the maples outside the Office Building were balls of brilliant carmine. The air was like crystal, and the landscape might have been bathed in liquid amber, it was so saturated with October yellow.

Susanna caught her breath as she threw her chamber window wider open in the early morning; for the greater part of the picture had been painted during the frosty night.

"Throw your little cape round your shoulders and come quickly, Sue!" she exclaimed.

The child ran to her side. "Oh, what a goldy, goldy morning!" she cried.

One crimson leaf with a long heavy stem that acted as a sort of rudder, came down to the window-sill with a sidelong scooping flight, while two or three gayly painted ones, parted from the tree by the same breeze, floated airily along as if borne on unseen wings, finally alighting on Sue's head and shoulders like tropical birds.

"You cried in the night, Mardie!" said Sue. "I heard you snifferling and getting up for your hank'chief; but I didn't speak 'cause it's so dreadful to be *catched* crying."

"Kneel down beside me and give me part of your cape," her mother answered. "I'm going to let my sad heart fly right out of the window into those beautiful trees."

"And maybe a glad heart will fly right in!" the child suggested.

"Maybe.—Oh! we must cuddle close and be still; Elder Gray's going to sit down under the great maple; and do you see, all the Brothers seem to be up early this morning, just as we are?"

"More love, Elder Gray!" called Issachar, on his way to the tool-house.

"More love, Brother Issachar!"

"More love, Brother Ansel!"

59

"More love, Brother Calvin!"

"More love!" "More love!" "More love!" So the quaint but not uncommon Shaker greeting passed from Brother to Brother; and as Tabitha and Martha and Rosetta met on their way to dairy and laundry and seed-house, they, too, hearing the salutation, took up the refrain, and Susanna and Sue heard again from the women's voices that beautiful morning wish, "More love!" "More love!" speeding from heart to heart and lip to lip.

Mother and child were very quiet.

"More love, Sue!" said Susanna, clasping her closely.

"More love, Mardie!" whispered the child, smiling and entering into the spirit of the salutation. "Let's turn our heads Farnham way! I'll take Jack and you take Fardie, and we'll say togedder, 'More love'; shall we?"

"More love, John."

"More love, Jack."

The words floated out over the trees in the woman's trembling voice and the child's treble.

"Elder Gray looks tired though he's just got up," Sue continued.

"He is not strong," replied her mother, remembering Brother Ansel's statement that the Elder "wa'n't diseased anywheres, but didn't have no durability."

"The Elder would have a lovely lap," Sue remarked presently.

"*What?*"

"A nice lap to sit in. Fardie has a nice lap, too, and Uncle Joel Atterbury, but not Aunt Louisa; she lets you slide right off; it's a bony, hard lap. I love Elder Gray, and I climbed on his lap one day. He put me right down, but I'm sure he likes children. I wish I could take right hold of his hand and walk all over the farm, but he wouldn't let me, I s'pose.—*More love, Elder Gray!*" she cried suddenly, bobbing up above the window-sill and shaking her fairy hand at him.

The Elder looked up at the sound of the glad voice. No human creature could have failed to smile back into the roguish face or have treated churlishly the sweet, confident little greeting. The heart of a real man must have an occasional throb of the father, and when Daniel Gray rose from his seat under the maple and called, "More love, child!" there was something strange and touching in his tone. He moved away from the tree to his morning labors with the consciousness of something new to conquer. Long, long ago he had risen victorious above many of the temptations that flesh is heir to. Women were his good friends, his comrades, his sisters; they no longer troubled the waters of his soul; but here was a child who stirred the depths; who awakened the potential father in him so suddenly and so strongly that he longed for the sweetness of a human tie that could bind him to her. But the current of the Elder's being was set towards sacrifice and holiness, and the common joys of human life he felt could never and must never be his; so he went to the daily round, the common task, only a little paler, a little soberer than was his wont.

"More love, Martha!" said Susanna when she met Martha a little later in the day.

"More love, Susanna!" Martha replied cheerily. "You heard our Shaker greeting, I see! It was the beautiful weather, the fine air and glorious colors, that brought the inspiration this morning, I guess! It took us all out of doors, and then it seemed to get into the blood. Besides, to-morrow's the Day of Sacrifice, and that takes us all on to the mountain-tops of feeling. There have been times when I had to own up to a lack of love."

"You, Martha, who have such wonderful influence over the children, such patience, such affection!"

"It wasn't always so. When I was first put in charge of the children, I didn't like the work. They didn't respond to me somehow, and when they were out of my sight they were ugly and disobedient. My natural mother, Maria Holmes, took care of the girls' clothing. One day she said to me, 'Martha, do you love the girls?'

"'Some of them are very unlovely,' I replied.

"'I know that,' she said, 'but you can never help them unless you love them.'

"I thought mother very critical, for I strove scrupulously to do my duty. A few days after this the Elder said to me: Martha, do you love the girls?' I responded, 'Not very much.'

"'You cannot save them unless you love them,' he said.

"Then I answered, 'I will labor for a gift of love.'

"When the work of the day was over, and the girls were in bed, I would take off my shoes and spend several hours of the night walking the floor, kneeling in prayer that I might obtain the coveted gift. For five weeks I did this without avail, when suddenly one night when the moon was full and I was kneeling by the window, a glory seemed to overshadow the crest of a high mountain in the distance. I thought I heard a voice say: '*Martha, I baptize you into the spirit of love!*' I sat there trembling for more than an hour, and when I rose, I felt that I could love the meanest human being that ever walked the earth. I have never had any trouble with children since that night of the vision. They seem different to me, and I dare say I am different to them."

"I wish I could see visions!" exclaimed Susanna. "Oh, for a glory that would speak to me and teach me truth and duty! Life is all mist, whichever way I turn. I'd like to be lifted on to a high place where I could see clearly."

She leaned against the frame of the open kitchen door, her delicate face quivering with emotion and longing, her attitude simplicity and unconsciousness itself. The baldest of Shaker prose turned to purest poetry when Susanna dipped it in the alembic of her own imagination.

"Labor for the gift of sight!" said Martha, who believed implicitly in spirits and visions. "Labor this very night."

It must be said for Susanna that she had never ceased laboring in her own way for many days. The truth was that she felt herself turning from marriage. She had lived now so long in the society of men and women who regarded it as an institution not compatible with the highest spiritual development that unconsciously her point of view had changed; changed all the more because she had been so unhappy with the man she had chosen. Curiously enough, and unfortunately enough for Susanna Hathaway's peace of mind, the greater aversion she felt towards the burden of the old life, towards the irksomeness of guiding a weaker soul, towards the claims of husband on wife, the stronger those claims appeared. If they had never been assumed!—Ah, but they had; there was the rub! One sight of little Sue sleeping tranquilly beside her; one memory of rebellious, faulty Jack; one vision of John, either as needing or missing her, the rightful woman, or falling deeper in the wiles of the wrong one for very helplessness;—any of these changed Susanna the would-be saint, in an instant into Susanna the wife and mother.

"*Speak to me for Thy Compassion's sake,*" she prayed from the little book of Confessions that her mother had given her. "*I will follow after Thy Voice!*"

"Would you betray your trust?" asked conscience.

"No, not intentionally."

"Would you desert your post?"

"Never, willingly."

"You have divided the family; taken a little quail bird out of the home-nest and left sorrow behind you. Would God justify you in that?"

For the first time Susanna's "No" rang clearly enough for her to hear it plainly; for the first time it was followed by no vague misgivings, no bewilderment, no unrest or indecision. "*I turn hither and thither; Thy purposes are hid from me, but I commend my soul to Thee!*"

Then a sentence from the dear old book came into her memory: "*And thy dead things shall revive, and thy weak things shall be made whole.*"

She listened, laying hold of every word, till the nervous clenching of her hands subsided, her face relaxed into peace. Then she lay down beside Sue, creeping close to her for the warmth and comfort and healing of her innocent touch, and, closing her eyes serenely, knew no more till the morning broke, the Sabbath morning of Confession Day.

X

I**F** Susanna's path had grown more difficult, more filled with anxieties, so had John Hathaway's. The protracted absence of his wife made the gossips conclude that the break was a final one. Jack was only half contented with his aunt, and would be fairly mutinous in the winter, while Louisa's general attitude was such as to show clearly that she only kept the boy for Susanna's sake.

Now and then there was a terrifying hint of winter in the air, and the days of Susanna's absence seemed eternal to John Hathaway. Yet he was a man about whom there would have been but one opinion: that when deprived of a rather superior and high-minded wife and the steadying influence of home and children, he would go completely "to the dogs," whither he seemed to be hurrying when Susanna's wifely courage failed. That he had done precisely the opposite and the unexpected thing, shows us perhaps that men are not on the whole as capable of estimating the forces of their fellow men as is God the maker of men, who probably expects something of the worst of them up to the very last.

It was at the end of a hopeless Sunday when John took his boy back to his aunt's towards night. He wondered drearily how a woman dealt with a ten-year-old boy who from sunrise to sunset had done every mortal thing he ought not to have done, and had left undone everything that he had been told to do; and, as if to carry out the very words of the church service, neither was there any health in him; for he had an inflamed throat and a whining, irritable, discontented temper that could be borne only by a mother, a father being wholly inadequate and apparently never destined for the purpose.

It was a mild evening late in October, and Louisa sat on the porch with her pepper-and-salt shawl on and a black wool "rigolette" tied over her head. Jack, very sulky and unresigned, was dispatched to bed under the care of the one servant, who was provided with a cupful of vinegar, salt, and water, for a gargle. John had more than an hour to wait for a returning train to Farnham, and although ordinarily he would have preferred to spend the time in the silent and unreproachful cemetery rather than in the society of his sister Louisa, he was too tired and hopeless to do anything but sit on the steps and smoke fitfully in the semi-darkness.

Louisa was much as usual. She well knew—who better?—her brother's changed course of life, but neither encouragement nor compliment were in her line. Why should a man be praised for living a respectable life? That John had

64

really turned a sort of moral somersault and come up a different creature, she did not realize in the least, nor the difficulties surmounted in such a feat; but she did give him credit secretly for turning about face and behaving far more decently than she could ever have believed possible. She had no conception of his mental torture at the time, but if he kept on doing well, she privately intended to inform Susanna and at least give her a chance of trying him again, if absence had diminished her sense of injury. One thing that she did not know was that John was on the eve of losing his partnership. When Jack had said that his father was not going back to the store the next week, she thought it meant simply a vacation. Divided hearts, broken vows, ruined lives—she could bear the sight of these with considerable philosophy, but a lost income was a very different, a very tangible thing. She almost lost her breath when her brother knocked the ashes from his meerschaum and curtly told her of the proposed change in his business relations.

"I don't know what I shall do yet," he said, "whether I shall set up for myself in a small way or take a position in another concern—that is, if I can get one—my stock of popularity seems to be pretty low just now in Farnham. I'd move away to-morrow and cut the whole gossipy, deceitful, hypocritical lot of 'em if I wasn't afraid of closing the house and so losing Susanna, if she should ever feel like coming back to us."

These words and the thought back of them were too much for John's self-control. The darkness helped him and his need of comfort was abject. Suddenly he burst out, "Oh, Louisa, for heaven's sake, give me a little crumb of comfort, if you have any! How can you stand like a stone all these months and see a man suffering as I have suffered, without giving him a word?"

"You brought it on yourself," said Louisa, in self-exculpation.

"Does that make it any easier to bear?" cried John. "Don't you suppose I remember it every hour, and curse myself the more? You know perfectly well that I'm a different man to-day. I don't know what made me change; it was as if something had been injected into my blood that turned me against everything I had liked best before. I hate the sight of the men and the women I used to go with, not because they are any worse, but because they remind me of what I have lost. I have reached the point now where I have got to have news of Susanna or go and shoot myself."

"That would be about the only piece of foolishness you haven't committed already!" replied Louisa, with a biting satire that would have made any man let go of the trigger in case he had gone so far as to begin pulling it.

"Where is she?" John went on, without anger at her sarcasm. "Where is she, how is she, what is she living on, is she well, is she just as bitter as she was at first, does she ever speak of coming back?—Tell me something, tell me anything. I will know something. I say I *will*!"

Louisa's calm demeanor began to show a little agitation, for she was not used to the sight of emotion.

"I can't tell you where Susanna is, for I made her a solemn promise I wouldn't unless you or Jack were in danger of some kind; but I don't mind telling you this much, that she's well and in the safest kind of a shelter, for she's been living from the first in a Shaker Settlement."

"Shaker Settlement!" cried John, starting up from his seat on the steps. "What's that? I know Shaker egg-beaters and garden-seeds and rocking-chairs and—oh, yes, I remember their religion's against marriage. That's the worst thing you could have told me; that ends all hope; if they once get hold of a woman like Susanna, they'll never let go of her; if they don't believe in a woman's marrying a good man, they'd never let her go back to a bad one. Oh, if I had only known this before; if only you'd told me, Louisa, perhaps I could have done something. Maybe they take vows or sign contracts, and so I have lost her altogether."

"I don't know much about their beliefs, and Susanna never explained them," returned Louisa, nervously, "but now that you've got something to offer her, why don't you write and ask her to come back to you? I'll send your letter to her."

"I don't dare, Louisa, I don't dare," groaned John, leaning his head against one of the pillars of the porch. "I can't tell you the fear I have of Susanna after the way I've neglected her this last year. If she should come in at the gate this minute, I couldn't meet her eyes; if you'd read the letter she left me, you'd feel the same way. I deserved it, to the last word, but oh, it was like so many separate strokes of lightning, and every one of them burned. It was nothing but the truth, but it was cut in with a sharp sword. Unless she should come back to me of her own accord, and she never will, I haven't got the courage to ask her; just haven't got the courage, that's all there is to say about it." And here John buried his head in his hands.

A very queer thing happened to Louisa Banks at this moment. A half-second before she would have murmured:—

"This rock shall flyFrom its firm base as soon as I!"

when all at once, and without warning, a strange something occurred in the organ she had always regarded—and her opinion had never been questioned—as a good, tough, love-tight heart. First there was a flutter and a tremor running all along her spine; then her eyes filled; then a lump rose in her throat and choked her; then words trembled on her tongue and refused to be uttered; then something like a bird—could it have been the highly respectable good-as-new heart?—throbbed under her black silk Sunday waist; then she grew like wax from the crown of her head to the soles of her feet; then in a twinkling, and so unconsciously as to be unashamed of it, she became a sister. You have seen a gray November morning melt into an Indian summer noon? Louisa Banks was like that, when, at the sight of a man in sore trouble, sympathy was born in her to soften the rockiness of her original make-up.

"There, there, John, don't be so down-hearted," she stammered, drawing her chair closer and putting her hand on his shoulder. "We'll bring it round right, you see if we don't. You've done the most yourself already, for I'm proud of the way you've acted, stiffening right up like an honest man and showing you've got some good sensible Hathaway stuff in you, after all, and ain't ashamed to turn your back on your evil ways. Susanna ain't one to refuse forgiveness."

"She forgave for a long time, but she refused at last. Why should she change now?" John asked.

"You remember she hasn't heard a single word from you, nor about you, in that out-of-the-way place where she's been living," said Louisa, consolingly. "She thinks you're the same as you were, or worse, maybe. Perhaps she's waiting for you to make some sign through me, for she don't know that you care anything about her, or are pining to have her back."

"Such a woman as Susanna must know better than that!" cried John. "She ought to know that when a man got used to living with anybody like her, he could never endure any other kind."

"How should she know all that? Jack's been writing to her and telling her the news for the last few weeks, though I haven't said a word about you because I didn't know how long your reformation was going to hold out; but I won't let the grass grow under my feet now, till I tell her just how things stand!"

"You're a good woman, Louisa; I don't see why I never noticed it before."

"It's because I've been concealing my goodness too much. Stay here with me to-night and don't go back to brood in that dismal, forsaken house. We'll see how Jack is in the morning, and if he's all right, take him along with you, so's to be all there together if Susanna comes back this week, as I kind of hope she will. Make Ellen have the house all nice and cheerful from top to bottom, with a good supper ready to put on the table the night she comes. You'd better pick your asters and take 'em in for the parlor, then I'll cut the chrysanthemums for you in the middle of the week. The day she comes I'll happen in, and stay to dinner if you find it's going to be mortifying for you; but if everything is as I expect it will be, and the way Susanna always did have things, I'll make for home and leave you to yourselves. Susanna ain't one to nag and hector and triumph over a man when he's repented."

John hugged Louisa, pepper-and-salt shawl, black rigolette, and all, when she finished this unprecedented speech; and when he went to sleep that night in the old north chamber, the one he and Louisa had been born in, the one his father and mother had died in, it was with a little smile of hope on his lips.

"Set her place at hearth and boardAs it used to be!"
These were the last words that crossed his waking thoughts.

Before Louisa went to her own bed, she wrote one of her brief and characteristic epistles to Susanna, but it did not reach her, for the "hills of home" had called John's wife so insistently on that Sunday, that the next day found her on her way back to Farnham.

DEAR SUSANNA [so the letter read],—There's a new man in your house at Farnham. His name is John Hathaway, but he's made all over and it was high time. *I* say it's the hand of God! He won't own up that it is, but I'm letting him alone, for I've done quarreling, though I don't like to see a man get religion and deny it, for all the world like Peter in the New Testament. If you haven't used up the last one of your seventy-times-sevens, I think you'd better come back and forgive your husband. If you don't, you'd better send for your son. I'm willing to bear the burdens the Lord intends specially *for* me, but Jack belongs to you, and a good-sized heavy burden he is, too, for his age. I can't deny that, if he *is* a Hathaway. I think he's the kind of a boy that ought to be put in a barrel and fed through the bung-hole till he grows up; but of course I'm not used to children's ways.

Be as easy with John at first as you can. I know you'll say *I* never was with *my* husband, but he was different. He got to like a bracing treatment, Adlai did. Many's the time he said to me, "Louisa, when you make up our minds, I'm always contented." But John isn't made that way. He's a changed man; now, what we've got to do is to *keep* him changed. He doesn't bear you any grudge for leaving him, so he won't reproach you.

Hoping to see you before long, I am,

Yours as usual,

Louisa Banks.

On the Saturday evening before the yearly Day of Sacrifice the spiritual heads of each Shaker family call upon all the Believers to enter heartily next day into the humiliations and blessings of open confession.

The Sabbath dawns upon an awed and solemn household. Footfalls are hushed, the children's chatter is stilled, and all go to the morning meal in silence. There is a strange quiet, but it is not sadness; it is a hush, as when in Israel's camp the silver trumpets sounded and the people stayed in their tents. "Then," Elder Gray explained to Susanna, "a summons comes to each Believer, for all have been searching the heart and scanning the life of the months past. Softly the one called goes to the door of the one appointed by the Divine Spirit, the human representative who is to receive the gift of the burdened soul. Woman confesses to woman, man to man; it is the open door that leads to God."

Susanna lifted Eldress Abby's latch and stood in her strong, patient presence; then all at once she knelt impulsively and looked up into her serene eyes.

"Do you come as a Believer, Susanna?" tremblingly asked the Eldress.

"No, Eldress Abby. I come as a child of the world who wants to go back to her duty, and hopes to do it better than she ever did before. She ought to be able to, because you have chastened her pride, taught her the lesson of patience, strengthened her will, purified her spirit, and cleansed her soul from bitterness and wrath. I waited till afternoon when all the confessions were over. May I speak now?"

Eldress Abby bowed, but she looked weak and stricken and old.

"I had something you would have called a vision last night, but I think of it as a dream, and I know just what led to it. You told me Polly Reed's story, and the little quail bird had such a charm for Sue that I've repeated it to her more than once. In my sleep I seemed to see a mother quail with a little one beside her. The two were always together, happily flying or hopping about under the trees; but every now and then I heard a sad little note, as of a deserted bird somewhere in the wood. I walked a short distance, and parting the branches, saw on the open ground another parent bird and a young one by its side darting hither and thither, as if lost; they seemed to be restlessly searching for something, and always they uttered the soft, sad note, as if the nest had disappeared and they had been parted from the little flock. Of course my brain had changed the very meaning of the Shaker story and translated it into different terms, but when I woke this morning, I could think of nothing but my husband and my boy. The two of them seemed to me to be needing me, searching for me in the dangerous open country, while I was hidden away in the safe shelter of the wood—I and the other little quail bird I had taken out of the nest."

"Do you think you could persuade your husband to unite with us?" asked Abby, wiping her eyes.

The tension of the situation was too tightly drawn for mirth, or Susanna could have smiled, but she answered soberly, "No; if John could develop the best in himself, he could be a good husband and father, a good neighbor and citizen, and an upright business man, but never a Shaker."

"Didn't he insult your wifely honor and disgrace your home?"

"Yes, in the last few weeks before I left him. All his earlier offenses were more against himself than me, in a sense. I forgave him many a time, but I am not certain it was the seventy times seven that the Bible bids us. I am not free from blame myself. I was hard the last year, for I had lost hope and my pride was trailing in the dust. I left him a bitter letter, one without any love or hope or faith in it, just because at the moment I believed I ought, once in my life, to let him know how I felt toward him."

"How can you go back and live under his roof with that feeling? It's degradation."

"It has changed. I was morbid then, and so wounded and weak that I could not fight any longer. I am rested now, and calm. My pluck has come back, and my strength. I've learned a good deal here about casting out my own devils; now I am going home and help him to cast out his. Perhaps he won't be there; perhaps he doesn't want me, though when he was his very best self he loved me dearly; but that was long, long ago!" sighed Susanna, drearily.

"Oh, this thing the world's people call love!" groaned Abby.

"There is love and love, even in the world outside; for if it is Adam's world it is God's, too, Abby! The love I gave my husband was good, I think, but it failed somewhere, and I am going back to try again. I am not any too happy in leaving you and taking up, perhaps, heavier burdens than those from which I escaped."

"Night after night I've prayed to be the means of leading you to the celestial life," said the Eldress, "but my plaint was not worthy to be heard. Oh, that God would increase our numbers and so revive our drooping faith! We work, we struggle, we sacrifice, we pray, we defy the world and deny the flesh, yet we fail to gather in Believers."

"Don't say you've failed, dear, dear Abby!" cried Susanna, pressing the Eldress's work-stained hands to her lips. "God speaks to you in one voice, to me in another. Does it matter so much as long as we both hear Him? Surely it's the hearing and the obeying that counts most! Wish me well, dear friend, and help me to say good-by to the Elder."

The two women found Elder Gray in the office, and Abby, still unresigned, laid Susanna's case before him.

"The Great Architect has need of many kinds of workmen in His building," said the Elder. "There are those who are willing to put aside the ties of flesh for the kingdom of heaven's sake; 'he that is able to receive it, let him receive it!'"

"There may also be those who are willing to take up the ties of the flesh for the kingdom of heaven's sake," answered Susanna, gently, but with a certain courage.

Her face glowed with emotion, her eyes shone, her lips were parted. It was a new thought. Abby and Daniel gazed at her for a moment without speaking, then Daniel said: "It's a terrible cross to some of the Brethren and Sisters to live here outside of the world, but maybe it's more of a cross for such as you to live in it, under such conditions as have surrounded you of late years. To pursue good and resist evil, to bear your cross cheerfully and to grow in grace and knowledge of truth while you're bearing it—that's the lesson of life, I suppose. If you find you can't learn it outside, come back to us, Susanna."

"I will," she promised, "and no words can speak my gratitude for what you have all done for me. Many a time it will come back to me and keep me from faltering."

She looked back at him from the open doorway, timidly.

"Don't forget us, Sue and me, altogether," she said, her eyes filling with tears. "Come to Farnham, if you will, and see if I am a credit to Shaker teaching! I shall never be here again, perhaps, and somehow it seems to me as if you, Elder Gray, with your education and your gifts, ought to be leading a larger life than this."

"I've hunted in the wild Maine forests, in my young days; I've speared salmon in her rivers and shot rapids in a birch-bark canoe," said the Elder, looking up from the pine table that served as a desk. "I've been before the mast and seen strange countries; I've fought Indians; I've faced perils on land and sea; but this Shaker life is the greatest adventure of all!"

"Adventure?" echoed Susanna, uncomprehendingly.

"Adventure!" repeated the Elder, smiling at his own thoughts. "Whether I fail, or whether I succeed, it's a splendid adventure in ethics."

Abby and Daniel looked at each other when Susanna passed out of the office door.

"'They went out from us, but they were not of us; for if they had been of us, they would have continued with us,'" he quoted quietly.

Abby wiped her eyes with her apron. "It's a hard road to travel sometimes, Daniel!" she said.

"Yee; but think where it leads, Abby, think where it leads! You're not going to complain of dust when you're treading the King's Highway!"

Susanna left the office with a drooping head, knowing the sadness she had left behind. Brother Ansel sat under the trees near by, and his shrewd eye perceived the drift of coming events.

"Well, Susanna," he drawled, "you're goin' to leave us, like most o' the other 'jiners.' I can see that with one eye shut."

"Yes," she replied, with a half smile; "but you see, Ansel, I 'jined' John Hathaway before I knew anything about Shaker doctrines."

"Yee; but what's to prevent your on-jinin' him? They used to tie up married folks in the old times so't they couldn't move an inch. When they read the constitution and by-laws over 'em they used to put in 'till death do us part.' That's the way my father was hitched to *his* three wives, but death *did* 'em part—fortunately for him!"

"'Till death us do part' is still in the marriage service," Susanna said, "and I think of it very often."

"I want to know if that's there yit!" exclaimed Ansel, with apparent surprise; "I thought they must be leavin' it out, there's so much on-jinin' nowadays! Well, accordin' to my notions, if there *is* anything wuss 'n marriage, it's hevin' it hold till death, for then men-folks don't git any chance of a speritual life till afterwards. They certainly don't when they're being dragged down by women-folks an' young ones."

"I think the lasting part of the bargain makes it all the more solemn," Susanna argued.

"Oh, yes, it's solemn enough, but so's a prayer meetin', an' consid'able more elevatin'"; and here Ansel regarded the surrounding scenery with frowning disapproval, as if it left much to be desired.

"Don't you think that there are *any* agreeable and pleasant women, Ansel?" ventured Susanna.

"Land, yes; heaps of 'em; but they all wear Shaker bunnits!"

"I suppose you know more about the women in the outside world than most of the Brothers, on account of traveling so much?"

"I guess anybody't drives a seed-cart or peddles stuff along the road knows enough o' women to keep clear of 'em. They'll come out the kitchen door, choose their papers o' seasonin' an' bottles o' flavorin', worry you 'bout the price an' take the aidge off every dime, make up an' then onmake their minds 'bout what they want, ask if it's pure, an' when by good luck you git your cart out o' the yard, they come runnin' along the road after ye to git ye to swop a bottle o' vanilla for some spruce gum an' give 'em back the change."

Susanna could not help smiling at Ansel's arraignment of her sex. "Do you think they follow you for the pleasure of shopping, or the pleasure of your conversation, Ansel?" she asked slyly.

"A little o' both, mebbe; though the pleasure's all on their side," returned the unchivalrousAnsel. "But take them same women, cut their hair close to their heads (there's a heap o' foolishness in hair, somehow), purge 'em o' their vanity, so they won't be lookin' in the glass all the time, make 'em depend on one another for sassiety, so they won't crave no conversation with men-folks, an' you git an article that's 'bout as good and 'bout as stiddy as a man!"

"You never seem to remember that men are just as dangerous to women's happiness and goodness as women are to men's," said Susanna, courageously.

"It don't seem so to me! Never see a man, hardly, that could stick to the straight an' narrer if a woman wanted him to go the other way. Weak an' unstable as water, men-folks are, an' women are pow'ful strong."

"Have your own way, Ansel! I'm going back to the world, but no man shall ever say I hindered him from being good. You'll see women clearer in another world."

"There'll be precious few of 'em to see!" retorted Ansel. "You're about the best o' the lot, but even you have a kind of a managin' way with ye, besides fillin' us all full o' false hopes that we'd gathered in a useful Believer, one cal'lated to spread the doctrines o' Mother Ann!"

"I know, I know, Ansel, and oh, how sorry I am! You would never believe how I long to stay and help you, never believe how much you have helped me! Good-by, Ansel; you've made me smile when my heart was breaking. I shan't forget you!"

SUSANNA had found Sue in the upper chamber at the Office Building, and began to make the simple preparations for her homeward journey.

It was the very hour when John Hathaway was saying:—

"Set her place at hearth and boardAs it used to be."
Sue interfered with the packing somewhat by darting to and fro, bringing her mother sacred souvenirs given her by the Shaker sisters and the children— needle-books, pin-balls, thimble-cases, packets of flower-seeds, polished pebbles, bottles of flavoring extract.

"This is for Fardie," she would say, "and this for Jack and this for Ellen and this for Aunt Louisa—the needle-book, 'cause she's so useful. Oh, I'm glad we're going home, Mardie, though I do love it here, and I was most ready to be a truly Shaker. It's kind of pityish to have your hair shingled and your stocking half-knitted and know how to say 'Yee' and then have it all wasted."

Susanna dropped a tear on the dress she was folding. The child was going home, as she had come away from it, gay, irresponsible, and merry; it was only the mothers who hoped and feared and dreaded.

The very universe was working toward Susanna's desire at that moment, but she was all unaware of the happiness that lay so near. She could not see the freshness of the house in Farnham, the new bits of furniture here and there; the autumn leaves in her own bedroom; her work-table full of the records of John's sorrowful summer; Jack handsomer and taller, and softer, also, in his welcoming mood; Ellen rosy and excited. She did not know that Joel Atterbury had said to John that day, "I take it all back, old man, and I hope you'll stay on in the firm!" nor that Aunt Louisa, who was putting stiff, short-stemmed chrysanthemums in cups and tumblers here and there through the house, was much more flexible and human than was natural to her; nor that John, alternating between hope and despair, was forever humming:—

"Set her place at hearth and boardAs it used to be;Higher are the hills of home,Bluer is the sea!"
It is often so. They who go weeping to look for the dead body of a sorrow, find a vision of angels where the body has lain.

"I hope Fardie'll be glad to see us and Ellen will have gingerbread," Sue chattered; then, pausing at the window, she added, "I'm sorry to leave the hills, 'cause I 'specially like them, don't you, Mardie?"

"We are leaving the Shaker hills, but we are going to the hills of home," her mother answered cheerily. "Don't you remember the Farnham hills, dear?"

"Yes, I remember," and Sue looked thoughtful; "they were farther off and covered with woods; these are smooth and gentle. And we shall miss the lake, Mardie."

"Yes; but we can look at the blue sea from your bedroom window, Sue!"

"And we'll tell Fardie about Polly Reed and the little quail bird, won't we?"

"Yes; but he and Jack will have a great deal to say to us, and we mustn't talk all the time about the dear, kind Shakers, you know!"

"You're all '*buts*,' Mardie!" at which Susanna smiled through her tears.

Twilight deepened into dusk, and dusk into dark, and then the moon rose over the poplar trees outside the window where Susanna and Sue were sleeping. The Shaker Brethren and Sisters were resting serenely after their day of confession. It was the aged Tabitha's last Sabbath on earth, but had she known, it would have made no difference; if ever a soul was ready for heaven, it was Tabitha's.

There was an Irish family at the foot of the long hill that lay between the Settlement and the village of Albion; father, mother, and children had prayed to the Virgin before they went to bed; and the gray-haired minister in the low-roofed parsonage was writing his communion sermon on a text sacred to the orthodox Christian world. The same moon shone over all, and over millions of others worshiping strange idols and holding strange beliefs in strange far lands, yet none of them owned the whole of heaven; for as Elder Gray said, "It is a big place and belongs to God."

Susanna Hathaway went back to John thinking it her plain duty, and to me it seems beautiful that she found waiting for her at the journey's end a new love that was better than the old; found a husband to whom she could say in that first sacred hour when they were alone together, "Never mind, John! Let's forget, and begin all over again."

. . . .

When Susanna and Sue alighted at the little railway station at Farnham, and started to walk through the narrow streets that led to the suburbs, the mother's heart beat more and more tumultuously as she realized that the issues of four lives would be settled before nightfall.

Little did Sue reck of life issues, skipping like a young roe from one side of the road to the other. "There are the hills, not a bit changed, Mardie!" she cried; "and the sea is just where it was!... Here's the house with the parrot, do you remember? Now the place where the dog barks and snarls is coming next.... P'raps he'll be dead ... or p'raps he'll be nicer.... Keep close to me till we get past the gate.... He didn't come out, so p'raps he is dead or gone a-visiting.... There's that 'specially lazy cow that's always lying down in the Buxtons' field.... I don't b'lieve she's moved since we came away.... Do you s'pose she stands up to be milked, Mardie? There's the old bridge over the brook, just the same, only the woodbine's red.... There's ... There's ... Oh, Mardie, look, look!... I do b'lieve it's our Jacky!"

Sue flew over the ground like a swallow, calling "Jack-y! Jack-y! it's me and Mardie come home!"

Jack extricated himself from his sister's strangling hug and settled his collar. "I'm awful glad to see you, Sukey," he said, "but I'm getting too big to be kissed. Besides, my pockets are full of angleworms and fishhooks."

"Are you too big to be kissed even by mother?" called Susanna, hurrying to her boy, who submitted to her embrace with better grace. "O Jack, Jack! say you're glad to see mother! Say it, say it; I can't wait, Jack!"

"Course I'm glad! why wouldn't I be? I tell you I'm tired of Aunt Louisa, though she's easier than she was. Time and again I've packed my lunch basket and started to run away, but I always made it a picnic and went back again, thinking they'd make such a row over me."

"Aunt Louisa is always kind when you're obedient," Susanna urged.

"She ain't so stiff as she was. Ellen is real worried about her and thinks she's losing her strength, she's so easy to get along with."

"How's ... father...?"

"Better'n he was."

"Hasn't he been well?"

"Not so very; always quiet and won't eat, nor play, nor anything. I'm home with him since Sunday."

"What is the matter with your clothes?" asked Susanna, casting a maternal eye over him while she pulled him down here and up there, with anxious disapproving glances. "You look so patched, and wrinkled, and grubby."

"Aunt Louisa and father make me keep my best to put on for you, if you should come. I clean up and dress every afternoon at train time, only I forgot to-day and came fishing."

"It's too cold to fish, sonny."

"It ain't too cold to fish, but it's too cold for 'em to bite," corrected Jack.

"Why were you expecting us just now?" asked Susanna. "I didn't write because, because, I thought ... perhaps ... it would be better to surprise you."

"Father's expecting you every day, not just this one," said Jack.

Susanna sank down on a stone at the end of the bridge, and leaning her head against the railing, burst into tears. In that moment the worst of her fears rolled away from her heart like the stone from the mouth of a sepulchre. If her husband had looked for her return, he must have missed her, regretted her, needed her, just a little. His disposition was sweet, even if it were thoughtless, and he might not meet her with reproaches after all. There might not be the cold greeting she had often feared—"*Well, you've concluded to come back, have you? It was about time!*" If only John were a little penitent, a little anxious to meet her on some common ground, she felt her task would be an easier one.

"Have you got a pain, Mardie?" cried Sue, anxiously bending over her mother.

"No, dear," she answered, smiling through her tears and stretching a hand to both children to help her to her feet. "No, dear, I've lost one!"

"I cry when anything aches, not when it stops," remarked Jack, as the three started again on their walk.—"Say, Sukey, you look bigger and fatter than you did when you went away, and you've got short curls 'stead of long ones.—Do you see how I've grown?—Two inches!"

"I'm inches and inches bigger and taller," Sue boasted, standing on tiptoe and stretching herself proudly. "And I can knit, and pull maple candy, and say Yee, and sing 'O Virgin Church, how great thy light.'"

"Pooh," said Jack, "I can sing 'A sailor's life's the life for me, Yo ho, yo ho!' Step along faster, mummy dear; it's 'most supper time. Aunt Louisa won't scold if you're with me. There's the house, see? Father'll be working in the garden covering up the asters, so they won't freeze before you come."

"There is no garden, Jack. What do you mean?"

"Wait till you see if there's no garden! Hurrah! there's father at the window, side of Aunt Louisa. Won't he be pleased I met you halfway and brought you home!"

Oh! it was beautiful, the autumn twilight, the smoke of her own hearthside rising through the brick chimneys! She thought she had left the way of peace behind her, but no, the way of peace was here, where her duty was, and her husband and children.

The sea was deep blue; the home hills rolled softly along the horizon; the little gate that Susanna had closed behind her in anger and misery stood wide open; shrubs, borders, young hedge-rows, beds of late autumn flowers greeted her eyes and touched her heart. A foot sounded on the threshold; the home door opened and smiled a greeting; and then a voice choked with feeling, glad with welcome, called her name.

Light-footed Sue ran with a cry of joy into her father's outstretched arms, and then leaping down darted to Ellen, chattering like a magpie. Husband and wife looked at each other for one quivering moment, and then clasped each other close.

"Forgive! O Susanna, forgive!"

John's eyes and lips and arms made mute appeals, and it was then Susanna said, "Never mind, John! Let's forget, and begin all over again!"